AGATHA ANXIOUS

& THE BACK BAY HAUNTING

Wyatt & Sons Publishers books may be ordered through booksellers or by contacting:

Wyatt & Sons Publishers, LLC
Mobile, Alabama 36695
www.wyattpublishing.com
editor@wyattpublishing.com

ISBN 13:978-1-954798-38-0
Printed in the United States of America

AGATHA ANXIOUS

& THE BACK BAY HAUNTING

RJ McDOWELL

Book 2 of **The Deadfellow Five**

WYATT & SONS
PUBLISHERS, LLC
Mobile, Alabama

For Clay.

Glory be, Mental Twin.

And for Timothy Guy.

O' Captain, My Captain.

***Krewe** [kroo]: noun – (in the US) an organization or association that stages a parade or other event for a carnival celebration. Krewes are associated especially with Mardi Gras.*

***Fleur-de-lis** [flur duh lee] a stylized lily or iris commonly used for decoration. Translated from French, it means 'lily flower.' The symbol has three petals attached at a base.*

-Oxford Languages

PROLOGUE

Lucius Nikolai drummed his grey fingers against the velvet fabric of his favorite chair, displeased. "Such a danger for you to visit me here. You know better."

A nod came from his visitor who faced him in one of the funeral home's wingback chairs. Warmth from the fireplace enveloped them both, though neither could feel it.

"You do understand you're not strong enough? Yet." Nikolai emphasized the "t" with a flick of his forked tongue.

Another nod accompanied by a snarly whisper. "Why? Why do you help her..."

Nikolai produced a small, glass vial from the pocket of his waistcoat and jiggled it, the thick liquid inside sticking to the sides of the glass, momentarily staining it red. "She keeps me here, in the land of the living." He motioned around him. "You know this." He tucked the vial back into his pocket and kept his bony hand on it, indicative of its importance. Guarding it.

Nikolai leaned in, the ashy skin of his nose nearly touching his companion's nose. Or the cavity where a nose should've been. "So, as I see it, we both need something from her."

"How..." Nikolai's companion coughed, a guttural, dry exhale of brown dust. "What...do I need?"

"An invitation, my dear." Nikolai smirked and leaned back into the soft velvet tufts of the chair. He rubbed his palms together, delightedly devising an evil plan. "You need an invitation."

CHAPTER 1
THE SUMMONING

Tippy Trinkle slid her tiny body out from between her silken sheets until her toes touched her carpet. She knelt beside her four-poster bed, pulling a small wooden box out from the darkness. As her fingers touched the initials on the box's top, she chewed her lip, deciding whether to proceed. Reaching under the bed again, she pulled out a small stash of items she'd hidden after breakfast that morning, items sure to garner her a punishment if her mother knew of their existence: a small candle, a set of matches, and a leatherbound little book titled J. Wiltz's Guide for Summoning the Dead.

She'd found the book at the weird gift shop on the beach. Hattie's Odds & Ends or something like that, although Tippy knew it was no longer run by Ms. Hattie. Instead, it was managed by Agatha Anxious' other aunt, the more serious one, whatever her name was.

Tippy didn't have money for the book, but she'd found an item under two dollars and being a master of distraction, had chatted up the aunt at the checkout—Aunt Less Friendly—as she'd slyly slipped the book in the waistband of her jeans. Now fingering its worn cover, Tippy felt a pang of regret for stealing it. Short-lived it was though, as she decided her purpose outweighed the crime.

She chose to sit in her closet, since it offered no light. Tippy lived in one of the old antebellum homes on Biloxi Beach, and the moonlight reflected off the water, making her bedroom far too bright for a task such as hers. Two strikes against the side of the matchbox and her candle flickered to life, its wooden wick crackling and sparking in the darkness. "Dark Library," the candle was called, and it smelled as musty as its title suggested. Another small trinket she took from Hattie's Odds & Ends.

Tippy studied the cover of the book. She wondered where it had been during its lifetime, and how many souls it had summoned back to the earth. Awakened from their coffin slumbers for purposes only known to the summoner.

What is my purpose? Tippy asked herself. For the last month, the ache of wanting to see her twin again nearly consumed her. Hardly any of Tippy's friends knew she'd had a twin. It wasn't something she discussed. But every now and then, and more often than she expected, the want of communication was so strong, she could hardly stand it.

It started three weeks ago when she'd found the toy. A pair of hugging pandas whose hands were magnetic and could be separated or attached. Most often, the pandas were separated. Her twin had one, and Tippy had the other. Tippy had begged to have one panda placed in the coffin at the funeral home, but her mother had refused and kept them both in her room, long forgotten by Tippy until recently when she found them in her mother's closet. Since then, the need to see her twin had been nearly unbearable.

Tippy opened the book to the table of contents and scanned until she saw "The Act of Summoning" chapter, deciding she didn't need to read all the fluff chapters before it. Let's get to it, she thought.

She skimmed the chapter, hitting the important steps and closed the book with a thud. Opening the wooden box, she pulled out a few of her twin's belongings she'd saved. A poem on notebook paper, a favorite book, a t-shirt, the panda, and lastly, his birth and death certificates, both of which she'd stolen from her father's office. She was getting good at stealing things.

"Henry Trinkle," she said. The candle crackled behind her whisper. She held her hand over the open flame until it hurt, immediately placing her open palm on the book.

"November seventh," she said. (Birthday)

"June eleventh." (Death date)

"February twenty-first." (Today's date)

"I want to see you." (Reason for summoning)

Silence.

She repeated it twice more, each time holding her palm over the open flame until it hurt. "November seventh. June eleventh. February twenty-first. I want to see you. November seventh. June eleventh. February twenty-first. I want to see you." And with a breath, she extinguished the candle.

Darkness enveloped her like a cloak, and she sat perfectly still, the white noise of nothingness loud in her ears. Tippy listened for any sign but was met with silence. She sat cross legged in the dark turning the matchbox over and over in between her fingers.

"Henry?" she whispered.

The air seemed to change in the small space of the closet. A rusty hanger above her shifted ever so slightly, scraping metal on metal, and she felt one of her hanging dresses brush her shoulder.

"Henry?" she said again, louder, fumbling to light a single match. The flame overtook the darkness, and Tippy saw she was alone. "Forget it," she huffed, throwing everything back in the wooden box. She kicked open the closet door with her foot and tossed the matches in the garbage can under her desk. With a sigh, she slid back into bed, throwing the covers over her head.

Tippy Trinkle lay on her back, deep in thought, her eyes clenched shut until she fell asleep, unaware of the evil which crept from the closet like a mist, floating through her bedroom, fingering the heavy fabric of her curtains, rustling the pages of the journal on her nightstand until it came to settle under the bed with an angry, little growl.

CHAPTER 2
AN OLD FRIEND

All January, Agatha Anxious left her Scrabble board out on her desk, directly and neatly in the center, a yellow plastic cup next to it filled with lettered tiles. She checked it daily, sometimes twice, but no message filled the plastic square-shaped divots of the game board.

Most of February was met with the same silence, and Agatha wondered when or if her next assignment would happen. Surely another ghost or ghoul would need assistance. After all, four glass pieces remained before Blanche Caillavet's hand mirror would be complete.

And then the wet winds of Friday, February 22nd arrived and with them, a storm.

"What a way to start Mardi Gras break," Agatha muttered to herself, as she gathered her books at the end of the school day and knelt before her locker. The covers on several of them, made from folded paper bags, were torn and bunched making it harder to cram everything in the small space. Agatha shoved the books with the heel of her palm, simultaneously knocking over a small cup of pens and pencils which hit the floor beside her knees. She sighed with her bottom lip, her breath fluffing her crooked bangs and gathered the items before slamming her locker shut.

A Martin Luther King, Jr. poster on the wall caught her eye. February was Black History Month, and his was one of several posters lining the walls, quotes beneath each historical person's face, their profound words etched into American history. A large handmade sign beneath the posters read, "Pick a quote and LIVE it! Do one small act that exemplifies the quote and then write about your experience. Due Monday, March 4th." She scrunched her face.

"Guess you forgot about that assignment, eh?" Leopold Panic said from behind her, taking a swig from his water bottle.

"Why do teachers always assign projects over a holiday? Can't they let us enjoy our lives?" Agatha pulled out her phone and took a picture of each of the seven options.

"I don't think 'enjoy' is in their vocabulary," Leopold took another swig. "Who are you picking?"

"Dunno. Everybody's gonna pick MLK. That's too obvious." She studied each person's face, seeing which one would speak to her. Frederick Douglass, Rosa Parks, Sojourner Truth, Harriet Tubman, George Washington Carver, Bessie Coleman. The last one was the only one she didn't know, and she pointed to it. "Maybe her."

They walked toward the school's front entrance where the doors were propped open, the heavy rain splashing inside onto the tile floors. Agatha tiptoed around a puddle. "Do you need a ride?" she said to Leopold as her mother's green station wagon pulled up with Tobie already inside. He must've run from the high school next door.

Leopold shook his head. "Nah. I'm going to the library until it stops raining."

"I don't think they stay open until midnight," she laughed, breaking into a run toward the car.

Tobie propped open the car door as she approached, and she dove inside.

"Thanks," she said, noticing hardly a speck of rain on him and knowing his run was longer than hers. "Must be nice to not get wet."

"Thanks to my Abraham Lincoln legs," he smiled and patted his knees, referring to his six-foot-two height.

October Anxious, more appropriately called Tobie, was Aunt Letty's son, who was three years older than Agatha. When he and Aunt Letty arrived in late November, Agatha regarded these strangers with suspicion—an aunt and a cousin she'd never met. Their appearance was sudden and swift, with Aunt Letty immediately settling into Aunt Hattie's house and taking over her shop. In some ways, Agatha found it intrusive, but she reminded herself her father had asked Aunt Letty to help. Aunt Letty wasn't doing it because she *wanted* to.

Tobie had a quiet intensity about him, usually studying the room and watching his companions. Observatory rather than participatory. His eyes, though brown, reminded Agatha of Dorian Doom. Something existed behind those chocolatey orbs, a decade and a half of life of which she wasn't a part, really. Sixteen years unknown to Agatha Anxious. He was a mystery to her, and one she intended to uncover. Someday.

Beneath his stoic façade, every now and then a fantastic, witty sense of humor would show itself with a biting one liner or a cutting comeback, both of which warmed Agatha's icy exterior toward October Anxious. And over the last couple months, in place of the sibling she'd always wanted, Agatha decided a cousin would do just fine. Quirks and all.

In January, Tobie began living with Agatha's family so he could attend Biloxi High School during the week, and he stayed with Aunt Letty on the weekends. In the Anxious family, Biloxi High School was far favored over the neighboring—and rival—city's high school, Gulfport High. The last three generations of the family had attended BHS, and Tobie was no exception, even if it meant the Anxious family had to give up the third and final room in their already tiny home. On top of living with Agatha, six days of the week Tobie was also working at Hattie's Odds & Ends, and Agatha had come to appreciate having another member in their tight-knit family circle. For the time being, Tobie Anxious had been a great tool for taking Agatha's mind off losing Aunt Hattie.

Once home, Agatha took a quick nap while the rain pitter-pattered against her window, tears running down the glass in different directions according to the wind. She'd hoped to forget about the evening's upcoming plans. Her mother, Anita Anxious, had signed up for a couple ballroom dancing lessons and didn't want to go alone. She'd invited Agatha to go, which was less of an invite and more of a demand, Agatha thought, but the storm threatened their plans. Agatha crossed her fingers the lesson would be canceled.

A few laughs from the living room caught Agatha's attention, and she got out of bed, pressing her ear to her bedroom door. She heard her parents' voices mingling with Tobie's. "Dropped yer pocket!" he exclaimed, followed by several hearty laughs. Agatha smiled. Laughter wasn't heard within the walls of the Anxious home as of late.

The whereabouts of Aunt Hattie still plagued her parents—her father Sonny, especially—and it seemed she'd joined Uncle Tim as another somber cloud lurking around corner, looming in every room, weighting every conversation. Agatha had watched her father's vocabulary dwindle to four words of a most burdensome nature: *What happened to Harriet?* For a while, it was all he could talk about. But lately, he'd entered the phase where he didn't say anything at all. For now, Aunt Hattie was not up for discussion.

The amount of guilt Agatha carried knowing the whereabouts of Aunt Hattie and not being able to tell her father was immeasurable, though of course neither of her parents would believe her if she did. Agatha sometimes imagined how that conversation would go.

"Mom? Dad? So, um, I don't want you guys to be sad anymore. I know where Aunt Hattie is, and I know you'll find this hard to believe, but she's the cat who's been living in our house. A few months ago, an evil old lady ghost turned her into a cat. But don't worry! I have all this under control. I'm not sure if she'll ever be human again, but she's a great pet and she seems happy."

Agatha snorted. *Those who don't have the gift will never understand.* Aunt Hattie's words danced in her brain as she stood at the window facing her backyard, pinching a piece of her wiry blonde hair between two fingers until it squeaked.

Agatha was antsy. The fact was this: Aunt Hattie was a cat. Forever. The white feline with the black spiral on its chest—now named Hattie-Cat when her parents weren't around—spent every waking hour at Agatha's side, oddly content to sleep the day away, clean its paws or stare at Agatha with its fudgy brown eyes, offering no assistance whatsoever. Her stare was sometimes a glare, Agatha thought, and she wondered if Aunt Hattie was disappointed in her or had reluctantly come to terms with her new form.

Agatha rested her chin on her palm, scanning the contents of her backyard with a yawn. A homemade firepit where the Anxious family sometimes roasted marshmallows, a small shed where her father stored his lawn mower and weed eater, a rusty swing set she no longer used, and a clothesline since their dryer often didn't work.

Agatha's gaze drifted further toward the Old Biloxi Cemetery, past the chain link fence dividing her yard from where bodies lay silently in the earth.

And some not so silently, she thought.

She scanned the graves, the oaks with moss hanging so low it appeared to hug some of the headstones. A crack of lightning illuminated some of the marble angels, their shadows moving on the crypts behind them. From where Agatha stood, she could just barely make out the top of Uncle Tim's headstone.

The rain turned to a soft drizzle, but the thunder persisted. Agatha checked her watch. Almost six thirty. The ballroom dancing lesson started at seven and was only a few streets over. More than enough time to make it. She groaned.

Another crack of lightning revealed something orange out of the corner of her eye. She leaned closer to the windowpane, squinting to see through the darkness. She was sure nothing in the cemetery was orange, not even the faded silk flowers adorning some of the graves. She pressed her nose to the window, her breath hot and humid against the glass.

Suddenly, a movement. There, next to a leaning oak was a familiar face, with two brown eyes which stared intently into Agatha's, even from the distance between them. Desperation filled his glare, and he raised his hand to point at her as she stared in disbelief.

Agatha knew him well. A tuxedo. No shoes. Orange, curly hair. Years ago, they'd spent many hours together, wasting away summer afternoons, lazy weekends and evenings after school. An extra place had been set for him at the table each night. A blanket and pillow had been beside her bed at bedtime. He'd been with her nearly every day for six months. Until suddenly he wasn't. No explanation, no reason, not a word. When her dad asked her where he was, Agatha had responded, "He's dead."

Thunder boomed again, and she blinked, trying to make sure what she was seeing was real. The boy opened his mouth as if to scream, but no sound came from his lips, and he continued to point.

He's dead. Her harsh, matter of fact words rung in her ears from years ago. Perhaps those words were more truth than she could've imagined. Because the boy standing in front of her now, his mouth open in a silent scream, was her childhood imaginary friend.

Big.

CHAPTER 3
THE DANCE

"I know you're not looking forward to this," Anita Anxious told her daughter as she buckled herself in the driver's seat of the family's green station wagon. "But I appreciate you going. I've always wanted to learn ballroom dancing."

"It's fine, mom. It should be...*fun*." Agatha squeaked out that last word, wholly unconvincingly. She was thankful for the distraction, though, after what she'd just witnessed in the cemetery. Why would Big be visiting her again after all these years?

They arrived at the Biloxi Community Center just in time for the first part of instructions, which included finding a partner. A much older partner, she would soon discover, as every participant was over eighty years old. Agatha, completely annoyed to discover her mother couldn't be her partner, was sought out by the only old man without one: Mr. Carr.

Great, she thought. *I'm picked last at school AND at ballroom dancing lessons where everyone is nearly dead!*

She scolded herself for being so rude. Agatha had known Mr. Carr for a long time. He was one of her mother's regular customers at the restaurant, never ordering anything more than coffee and always carrying little trinkets or treats for Anita Anxious to bring home to her daughter. Gum, toy cars, gummy bears, pecan swirls, and shells.

He was the nicest old man with a most unfortunate affliction. Having been fond of tobacco for most of his life, Mr. Carr had been diagnosed with cancer a few years ago, and it had eaten through the tissue under his tongue. When he talked, his tongue protruded ever so slightly through the hole in his jaw beneath his bottom teeth. And now Agatha was face to face with him practicing silly waltz steps which had them moving in the shape of a square. At least they weren't touching. *Yet.* Maybe she could get out of next week's lesson. Maybe her mother would hate this and would never want to come back.

"One, two, three. One, two, three," the instructor repeated, clapping her hands and smiling. Her red lipstick was smudged on the left side of her lip and the eye above it drooped to match.

Mr. Carr reached for Agatha's hand with a smile as the instructor indicated it was now time to dance *with* partners. She gulped as the music started. His hand was cold, and she felt it shake as he attempted to close his fingers around hers, the soft buttery folds of his palm enveloping hers. He was gentle, and she wasn't as uncomfortable as she thought she'd be. He said nothing as they went through the few basic steps of the waltz they'd just learned.

She looked over at her mother who gave her the thumbs up sign and smiled. She seemed to be enjoying herself, and Agatha's heart sunk. After what seemed like forever, the music ended and to her surprise, everyone faced Agatha and clapped. She felt her cheeks burn under the weight of the attention.

"Very nice, young lady," the instructor nodded. "Impressive."

Impressive? What had she done? She'd danced in the shape of a square with a partner who'd practically led her the entire way. Not to mention she'd had to learn square dancing and Tinikling in elementary school P.E., and that was WAY harder.

Anita Anxious rushed over to her daughter but said nothing to Mr. Carr. "I'm a bit stunned you took to this so naturally! I'm just so—oh, hang on, love. There's Miss Eleanor, our old neighbor. Let me go have a chat. Meet you at the car." And she was gone before Agatha could respond.

The room emptied of its elderly dancers as Agatha turned to face Mr. Carr. "Thank you, Mr. Ca...." her voice hung on the vowel sound of his last name. Cradled in the pink wrinkles of his palms, he held out a small white jar, a black skull with wings embellishing its top. He turned it over to reveal what Agatha already knew would be adorning it: a sketch of a dead black tree on its side. A skull jar.

Her stomach seized with excitement. Agatha realized they were the only two people now remaining in the dance hall. "Thank you?" she said, her words delivered more like a question. She took the skull jar from his waiting hands and stuffed it into her crossbody black purse. Rushing to the door, she glanced back toward Mr. Carr.

"Thanks for the dance, Agatha," he said, his tongue rolling and wiggling in the soft fleshy opening of his jaw. "Be. Careful."

CHAPTER 4
A SECOND MESSAGE

Agatha paid no attention to her mother on the drive home. In fact, she couldn't recall one word she'd said. Once at the house, Agatha rushed to her room, dumping the contents of her small purse onto her bed. A pencil with a broken lead, a small flashlight, gum wrappers filled with chewed gum, her cell phone, two bitten pieces of black licorice, six quarters and one lone peppermint. And, last but not least, the skull jar. She picked it up between her thumb and middle finger, being just as careful as last time, and placed it on the top shelf in her closet. Closing the door behind her, she lay back on the bed. All the months of anticipation and now she was reluctant to open it, worried about who it was and what they'd need. Plus, there was the nagging feeling she didn't need to open the jar, really. *She knew who it was.*

"Agatha," her mother knocked on the door and opened it without waiting for a reply. "Don't forget you're helping Aunt Letty tomorrow at the shop."

"I haven't forgotten." How could she? As strange as Aunt Letty was, the shop made her feel close to Aunt Hattie.

"Tobie said he'd drive you after lunch, ok?"

Agatha's throat caught on some saliva. "In....in the truck?"

"Yep! In the truck." Anita Anxious was already halfway out the door with no intention of touching the topic.

A few weeks ago, shortly before entering the stage of not talking about Aunt Hattie, Agatha's father Sonny had gifted her truck to Tobie since he recently obtained his driver's license. It required repairs and was being fixed by one of her father's coworkers, and Agatha had largely been able to forget about the truck. Tobie offered to drive Agatha to school once it was ready, but she'd planned on finding different excuses to avoid being in it. The time had come though, it seemed, to face one of her fears.

"Mom, I can walk to the shop. The shop is not far."

"It's supposed to rain all day tomorrow, honey. Plus, Tobie is excited to drive." Her mother was now in the hallway. Agatha suspected she knew exactly what her daughter was trying to avoid. "Can't wait for our next dancing lesson!" she called, effectively ending the conversation.

Agatha turned out her lights, grabbed the jar and stood at her window. The grass had recently been mowed making all the graves look tidy. A small breeze moved the wind chime in the backyard, and it sang a foreboding three notes as Agatha grasped the skull handle and popped open the top of the jar, revealing a curled, white piece of paper. She gently pulled it from the jar and read the printed script, confirming exactly what she'd thought since seeing Big in the cemetery earlier that evening.

REMEMBER ME?

It was him, but what could he possibly want? He'd spoken to her years before as her imaginary friend and never seemed to want anything then, although Agatha was too young to even ask or know that he was dead. As she stuffed the note back into the jar, it caught on something. Peering inside she saw a second piece of paper. A second message. This one was crumpled, as if folded in a hurry and jammed into the jar. It was a poem, presumably from Big too. She recalled he'd been fond of poems, but the subjects of his writings had been often good natured, of clouds and summer and sunshine. This poem was reminiscent of absolutely none of that, and Agatha bit the inside of her cheek.

THERE ARE TWO OF ME.

THERE SHOULDN'T BE.

CHAPTER 5
DEAD IS DEAD

Agatha awoke late on Saturday with no time for a shower or food. She tried to run her fingers through her wiry hair, but they got caught in all different places, knotted up during the night as she tossed and turned with thoughts of Big. She gave up and pulled it all back with a black clip.

Maybe Aunt Letty will have some food at the shop, she thought, as she trudged through the cemetery on her way to Beach Boulevard. She purposely glanced over at Blanche Caillavet's crypt, wary, but unafraid. The angel still bowed in prayer out front, the iron gate still partially off its hinges. The cemetery light was on, as usual, and Agatha knew she wasn't just going to go away. No grey hand protruded from the door of the crypt this time, though. Altogether, the grave appeared unattended, unvisited, and sad. *No sympathy for you,* Agatha thought. Some graves didn't deserve visitors.

Agatha glanced at her uncle's grave, nodded, and proceeded to the beach.

The door rang above her head as she entered Hattie's Odds & Ends, the same bell Aunt Hattie had hung last year to keep her aware of Mr. Dominicus' comings and goings. She felt a pang of sadness every time she heard it. Both were now gone—Mr. Dominicus and Aunt Hattie—and sometimes remembering hurt a little too much.

Aunt Letty sat at the large wooden desk that was once her sister's, her blonde bob—much like Agatha's—protruding in all different directions as if she, too, hadn't gotten any sleep the night before. She tucked an untamed wisp behind her ear. "Hi, Agatha." Aunt Letty didn't do the Miz Magnolia game.

"Hi," Agatha said through a yawn.

"We match." Aunt Letty pointed to Agatha's clothes, a black long sleeve cotton dress with used black ankle boots her mother had found at the thrift store. Aunt Letty's attire was her usual black lace dress but hers ended at her ankles, not her knees like Agatha's.

"We always match, Auntie," Agatha grinned and caught herself. "I mean Aunt...Letty." "Auntie" was reserved for one person only.

The bell chimed again, signaling Leopold's entrance. "Good morning, Miss Letty," he said politely, always on cue with manners.

Recently, he'd begun helping at the shop a few days a week. With Mr. Dominicus gone—he could rest now knowing his grandson no longer bore the guilt of his death—the shop needed employees, and Letty didn't trust many people, if any.

Letty nodded in Leopold's direction, her slanted green eyes surveying him up and down. She scratched her chin. "There are a few boxes in the back to be unpacked, and you can sweep off the front porch. That's probably all I have for you today because Tobie did a lot this morning."

Agatha's shoulders slumped. She'd forgotten Tobie and the ride. Oh well. She'd gotten out of being in the truck.

"Agatha," she said, coming around from behind the desk with her hands on the curves of her hips, and Agatha could see she was barefoot. "You can straighten the items on the last row to the left. A couple of the booths need reorganizing and dusting." She handed her a feather duster.

Red Rum Row, she thought nervously. However, when Agatha got to the row, everything looked in order. Most days it seemed Aunt Letty was finding things for both she and Leopold to do. Unnecessary things. Did she really need this much help, or did she want them there for a particular reason?

Agatha spent the next hour dusting picture frames, organizing old books on shelves, and rearranging dried flowers in vases. As she moved from booth to booth, the lighting seemed to change. Agatha peered towards the last booth at the back. It was dark. In fact, the entire back of the store seemed to be in darkness.

"Aunt Letty!" she called.

"The lights at the back of the store are out, Agatha," Aunt Letty answered matter-of-factly. "Nothing to worry about."

How did she know? "I'm not scared," Agatha shot back.

"You sure? I can hear it in your voice." Tobie walked past her toward the shop's back room, returning momentarily with two boxes and a crooked smile. "There's no such things as ghosts, Agatha."

"You don't really believe that do you?"

"Believe what? That there AREN'T ghosts? Of course, I do. Dead is dead."

"You don't think things ever come back?"

Tobie reprimanded her with his eyes and cocked his head. "Pretty sure you should've learned this in science class a few years back at the very least."

Agatha kept her eyes locked on him. "So, all the stuff in this store, on this row especially, none of it bothers you? You don't think any of this is creepy?"

Tobie ignored her and turned to leave, walking backwards while balancing the boxes in the crook of one arm. "The lights went out at the back of the store earlier this morning. It's dark, but you're alone, Agatha."

Agatha stared again at the last booth on the row. "I'm never alone in the dark," she whispered.

She approached booth 14 cautiously, tiptoeing as much as the rigid leather of her boots would allow, finding it nearly in complete darkness. Agatha let her eyes adjust before proceeding. The booth held a bit of foreboding for Agatha as the home and final resting place of a life size knight in a suit of armor. Aunt Hattie acquired the knight years ago, but no one ever bought it, which Agatha attributed to less of customers' disinterest and more of Aunt Hattie's desire to keep it. Now it was nothing more than a decoration, only adding to the evil aura of the booth.

As she worked her way through the items, something crunched beneath Agatha's boot. A large glass dish, broken into several pieces, lay in a pile on the floor, as if purposely stomped or smashed into the thin carpet. Agatha bent to collect the pieces, carefully collecting the shards between her thumb and forefinger, to avoid cutting her fingertips. She squinted in the darkness, trying to find them all.

"Who did this?" After picking up the third piece, she noticed more tiny fragments from several other glass items led away from the first pile, straight toward the knight as if in a direct line to the looming figure. At his feet was yet another pile of broken pieces, but this time, they were numerous and deliberately spelled a message. Agatha froze, knowing she would have to get near the knight in order to read it. She wondered about any alternatives and looked around.

"Leopold?" Agatha whispered.

"He's sweeping the porch, Agatha," Aunt Letty called from the front desk. How did she hear her?

"It's a special thing to be a Perceiver," Agatha whispered to herself as she got on her hands and knees. She inched toward the final pile of glass, a full sentence spelled out in capital letters, perfect and precise. She didn't want to get too close.

SHE DOESN'T KNOW WHAT SHE'S DONE

As she arched her neck to read the message, a movement from between the knight's feet caught her eye. Agatha shifted her gaze and saw two small feet. Ten little toes were attached to the two feet, then two legs clothed in black pants attached to a torso in a tuxedo. Agatha's eyes followed the body all the way up to two familiar eyes, wild with despair and aching to speak, though he didn't.

A wave of fear trickled from her neck to her toes, and Agatha dug her fingers into the carpet as Big peeked from behind the knight. He crouched to Agatha's level and Agatha saw in the darkness he was shivering.

HELP, he mouthed.

CHAPTER 6
MONEY FOR YOUR TROUBLE

Agatha made no mention of the events in booth 14 on Red Rum Row as she prepared to leave the store that evening. Regardless, Aunt Letty stopped her and Leopold on their way out.

"Do either of you know a girl with very long dark black hair?"

Leopold looked at Agatha, waiting for her to answer. She could only mean Tippy. Although there were several kids in school with black hair, only one of them had hair of Tippy's color. A deep, dark, almost unnatural black. Plus, it was longer than anybody else's.

"I think you mean, Tippy Trinkle," Agatha said. "Long, straight black hair? Like, long. To her waist?"

Aunt Letty nodded. "Yes, and a lot of makeup. Dark, thick, overdone eyebrows. Long eyelashes. Too much for a girl her age. Do you know where she lives?"

"Yes," said Leopold. Now he was interested.

"She was in here a couple days ago," Aunt Letty started.

"She was?" Agatha interrupted, finding it hard to believe Tippy Trinkle would ever have a reason to be in a weird, eclectic shop like Hattie's Odds & Ends. Most kids their age didn't shop at antique/oddity type stores.

Aunt Letty narrowed her eyes at Agatha. "Yes. And she stole a couple things, one of which I want back."

"She *stole* something?" Leopold was super fascinated now.

"Why is this hard to believe?" Aunt Letty looked at Agatha and Leopold and then back to Agatha.

"Well, she just has lots of money," said Leopold. "Like, she wouldn't just pay for whatever it was?"

"Perhaps because of *what* it was."

"What was it, Aunt Letty?" Agatha nibbled the side of one of her thumbs. She was ready to leave.

Aunt Letty circled back to the counter, situating herself behind the cash register. "You'll find out when you go to retrieve it at her house. I assume she lives within a short distance since she arrived on a bike. Tobie can give you a ride."

"You want us to go to her house and retrieve something you think she stole?" said Agatha. She was more unnerved by the fact that she'd now have to ride in Aunt Hattie's truck.

Aunt Letty licked two of her fingers and tucked another wisp of hair behind her ear, patting it down with the saliva until it obeyed. She turned to the register, pressing a few buttons until the cash drawer opened. "I don't *think* she stole it, Agatha. I *know* she did." She handed

Agatha a one-hundred-dollar bill. "Split this between you both for your trouble."

Tobie jingled the bell of the door with his hand, his tall thin frame allowing him easy access to the top parts of the door. "Let's go, losers. I have things to do."

"Like what?" said Agatha. "You don't have any friends."

"True. I like it that way," he winked.

Aunt Letty cleared her throat loudly and plopped herself behind the large wooden desk with a sigh. She turned her back as if to tell them all she was done with them. "Have a good night."

CHAPTER 7

A FACE WITH A NAME

"A hundred dollars?" Leopold said excitedly as they drove toward Tippy's house on the beach. "We're rich!"

Agatha stared straight through the windshield, smushed between Tobie and Leopold. The truck still smelled of Aunt Hattie, an intoxicating scent of patchouli, incense, and flowers mingled with magic and her own sadness, and Agatha wanted to puke.

"We're not rich," Agatha said, distracting herself. "Whatever Tippy stole must be pretty important to Aunt Letty. Enough to give us a hundred dollars for it." She was already on edge because of Big in booth 14 and now having to ride in the truck. Truthfully, she just wanted to be home in her bed. "It makes me suspicious."

"You guys do know you're talking about my mom, right? And I'm sitting like, right here." Tobie ran a hand through his brown hair, which was touching the truck's ceiling. Where Aunt Hattie had looked like a child behind the wheel sitting on her oversized pillow, Tobie seemed like a giant.

"It's right up here." Leopold directed and Tobie flipped on the blinker, slowing to a crawl as they entered Tippy Trinkle's driveway leading to her mammoth home.

Tippy's mansion, as Agatha liked to call it, was a large two-story structure facing the gulf water, with two fireplaces and lots of white columns which seemed to announce, "Hey we have a lot of money" to any passersby on Biloxi Beach. Agatha saw both floors of the home had a wraparound porch with rocking chairs. She counted four apiece on each porch.

"Ugh, I hope this is quick."

"Hey, we get to go inside Tippy Trinkle's house! This would never happen in a million years. I've always wondered what the inside looked like," Leopold said, exiting the truck.

"You think she's going to invite us in after we accuse her of stealing something from my aunt? Come on. I mean what are we even gonna say?" Agatha scowled, scooting across the seat. Before shutting the truck's door, she pleaded with Tobie to accompany them.

"You see where my butt is sitting right now?"

Agatha rolled her eyes, knowing what he was going to say.

"It's going to continue to sit right here until y'all are through." He smiled big.

Leopold was already on the porch. "I got this," he said when Agatha joined him, clearing his throat and ringing the doorbell. "Follow my lead."

No one came to the door, and Leopold rang it again. "Dang. Maybe they're not home," he said, clearly disappointed.

"Um, hi?"

Leopold and Agatha looked around.

"Up here."

They stepped off the front porch and saw Tippy standing on the second story balcony. "What's up?" Agatha detected a suspicious tone in her voice.

Leopold froze. A few milliseconds of uncomfortable silence boomeranged between the three schoolmates until Agatha spoke.

"Um, we were in the neighborhood...well, this isn't a neighborhood since you actually live on the beach...area, I guess? Yeah, we were in the area and thought we'd say hi? Maybe we can come in and have a chat?" Agatha closed her eyes. Have a chat? Her grandmother used to say things like that. Old people-y things. She gritted her teeth and elbowed Leopold.

"Yeah, we were just kind of bored and we happened to be passing by." Leopold found his voice again.

Tippy stared like she didn't believe either of them. "Alright," she shrugged, disappearing into the house.

Leopold looked at Agatha, rubbing his hands together excitedly and smiling like a fool.

"Oh, stop it," she muttered. "We're about to accuse her of stealing."

The heavy wooden front door swung open, and Tippy motioned for them to enter. She pointed to a small sign right inside the front door: *"Please take off your shoes. And don't take a better pair when you leave!"*

"Oh," Agatha said, while Leopold set about untying his sneakers. She squatted inside the front door and reluctantly removed her boots. Both of her socks had holes in them, and she avoided Tippy's eyes to see if she had seen. Her cheeks were hot with shame, but thankfully Tippy was facing Leopold.

A circular staircase immediately greeted Agatha and Leopold, and Agatha tried to hide her amazement. She'd read about circular staircases but hadn't seen one in person. Black and white tile flooring was everywhere, and it led them from room to room like following a trail. *Breadcrumbs,* Agatha thought. She wondered if she and Leopold were Hansel and Gretel, and Tippy was the witch about to shove them into her gigantic oven after they told her she was a thief.

Tippy gave an unenthusiastic tour. "Everybody always wants to see the house," she said flatly. They followed her through a sitting room complete with a large stone fireplace that would've thrilled Santa Claus. A library with hundreds of books, a desk, and three couches. *Who has three couches?* One large bedroom where Tippy closed the door. "My parents' room," she said, leading them in another direction to a completely brick room.

"What's this room for?"

"It's a mudroom. Ya know, for taking off shoes, hanging coats, or washing a dirty dog."

Agatha's eyes followed the shower head on one wall down to an attached hose beneath it and a drain in the floor. She realized her mouth was open in disbelief and she closed it.

"So, how many dogs you have?" Leopold asked.

"None," Tippy said without missing a beat.

They ended the first floor showing in the kitchen, surrounded by white marble countertops, silver fixtures, and a double oven. Copper pots and pans of every size hung from hooks above the stove, which was situated on a large marble island directly in the center of the room. Tippy motioned for them to take a seat at one of the six island barstools.

"I'd ask you if you want something to drink, but we don't have much. And I'm thinking I probably should ask why you're here first. Neither of you are ever 'in the neighborhood.'" Tippy popped the top on a soda and served herself.

Leopold looked at Agatha. "All yours."

"Oh, thanks," Agatha said under her breath. She cleared her throat, but her voice came out far less commanding and direct than she'd hoped.

"Tippy, did you go to my aunt's shop recently?"

Tippy sipped her cola without answering.

"My..." Agatha's voice caught in her throat. "My Aunt Letty asked us to come by." It was the nicest way to put it. If Tippy had taken something, she'd know exactly what Agatha meant.

Tippy looked at Leopold, who shrugged. She slurped her cola once more and abruptly left the room. They could hear her bounding up the spiral staircase. After a few minutes, Leopold looked at Agatha. "Should we just leave?"

"No. She knows."

Tippy reappeared in the kitchen, her black hair now tied in a bun. She was sweating. "Here." She tossed an old little book in their direction, and it landed face down in front of Leopold. "I forgot to pay for it."

Agatha doubted Tippy's words but wondered about Aunt Letty sending them on a mission for a tattered old book. "Ok.," she said, grabbing it. "Well, this went better than I expected," she smiled nervously.

"Does she want the candle and matches back too?" Tippy asked. "I kind of like those."

Leopold laughed, scooting in the barstool. "Did you forget to pay for all of those things?"

Tippy rolled her eyes. "No, I just...Fine. I needed those things, and I didn't have any money."

Leopold raised an eyebrow.

"Just because I have a big house doesn't mean I—ME personally—doesn't mean I have any money, you know."

He held his hands up. "Ok."

"What do you mean you *needed* the items?" Agatha questioned. She turned the book over in her hands to reveal its title, the gold cursive lettering missing in the curvatures of some the letters. *J. Wiltz's Guide for Summoning the Dead.* Her heart stopped.

She looked hard at Tippy. "You needed this?"

"It doesn't work anyway," Tippy said, popping the top on another soda.

"I thought you didn't have any drinks?" Leopold said. Agatha shot him a look.

"What do you mean it doesn't work? Did you use this book?"

"Well duh," said Tippy. "I tried. That's what I mean by it didn't work. Nothing happened." She wiped some of the sweat from her brow with the back of her hand.

"Did you try to summon...someone?"

Tippy lowered her hand from her face, suddenly serious. She looked at her feet, ten perfectly painted purple toenails on two petite feet. She wiggled her right foot nervously. "My brother."

"You have a brother?" Both Agatha and Leopold spoke simultaneously.

Tippy gnawed the inside of her cheek still staring at her toes. "Had."

Leopold couldn't help himself. "What happened to him? He died?"

"Well of course he died, Leopold! I'm sorry," Agatha said to Tippy. "Don't answer that."

"No, it's ok," Tippy continued. "No one ever asks, so it's ok to talk about him sometimes. He died about six years ago at the hospital on Back Bay. We were twins."

Leopold sucked in a breath. "Oh my God, really?"

Tippy looked up. "Yes, I had a twin."

"No, the Back Bay Hospital? As in, the haunted hospital everybody sneaks into and tries to spend the night in?"

"Leopold—" Agatha started.

"Yeah, the abandoned one," Tippy said, unbothered.

Leopold switched topics. "How did he die?"

Agatha elbowed Leopold. "Stop it," she whispered.

"Seriously," Tippy looked at Agatha. "It's fine. We got really sick when we were younger. Both of us went into the hospital." She paused. "And only one of us came out."

All three were quiet while Tippy's refrigerator hummed in the background. Somewhere in the house, a clock chimed four times, announcing the hour.

"I try to talk to him sometimes, which is why I wanted the book. When I saw it at your aunt's shop, I knew I needed it, but I didn't have the money."

Agatha understood this to be Tippy's apology without saying so.

"Do you have a picture of your brother?" said Leopold, clearly still intrigued by the dead sibling story. "What?" he mouthed to Agatha under her glare.

"Yes. All our family pictures are at the top of the staircase. My mom only keeps one picture of Henry out—that was his name, by the way. Henry. Everything else is in a box somewhere." She motioned for them to follow her.

Tippy turned, leading them back through the library toward the spiral staircase and up the curved stairs. Agatha studied the back of Tippy's head and the underpart of her raven hair, now showing in the bun she'd fashioned a few minutes prior. A few dainty curls bounced lazily against the back of her neck, and she wondered if Tippy's hair was naturally curly. Curly-haired girls always wanted straight hair and straight-haired girls always wanted curly hair. Agatha patted down her own hair wondering what it currently looked like. Where was a mirror in this castle?

Leopold followed Tippy to the landing while Agatha studied the family portraits as she climbed the stairs, zeroing in on how different every member of the Trinkle family looked. Tippy's father was blonde, and thin and tall like Tobie. Her mother had reddish hair, cut in a shoulder length bob, and she appeared short compared to her husband. The top of her head did not meet his shoulders in several of the family pictures. Agatha paused in front of an old photograph of a child with bright orange curly hair and lots of freckles. The child was smiling, caught in the middle of a laugh, exposing a small gap between its front teeth.

She jammed the corner of her pinky in between her front teeth. "Who...is this?" she stammered, her heart starting to pound. She could hear it from where she stood.

Tippy arched her neck to see what Agatha what staring at. "Oh, that's my mom when she was a baby." Tippy turned back toward Leopold, having reached the top of the stairs. "Here he is," Agatha heard her say, pointing to one large, framed picture hanging by itself against the grey wall.

Leopold leaned in, studying the photograph. "Wow. Y'all don't really look alike."

"Yeah, not really. Fraternal twins. Obviously," Tippy replied.

"I didn't know twins could have completely different hair colors," said Leopold, intrigued.

Agatha bit the skin inside her lip until she tasted blood, climbing the stairs in slow motion toward the photograph containing a face she knew she would recognize. She stopped next to Leopold and pretended to look at the picture, her gaze several inches to the right of the frame. "Wow," she said, feigning interest.

"My mom keeps his room the same as it was years ago. We don't go in there, though," Tippy said. She pointed down the hallway toward the last room on the right. "My room's up here though if you want to see it. May as well get the candle I took. Your Aunt can have that back I guess."

Leopold was already on the landing, anxious to explore the rest of the mansion.

"I'll..." Agatha swallowed, "...be there in a second."

"Ok," said Tippy, disappearing with Leopold.

Agatha looked at her socks, the middle toe of her right foot unpainted and protruding through a hole. She curled it under, wriggling it back into the black fabric of the sock so she wouldn't have to look at it. A bad taste filled her mouth, and she swallowed it away as she looked at the portrait. A warmth spread from her neck and chest down to her tummy and out along her arms to her fingertips where it fanned out into a vicious tingle. She held her breath.

The boy staring back at her finally had a name after all these years. A name, a home, and a family. A real family. Agatha had known him all along, and now maybe she would have the answers to the many questions about who he really was, what he wanted back then and most importantly, what he needed now.

She clasped her tingling hands together at her chest and looked away. His name wasn't Big. It was Henry Trinkle.

CHAPTER 8
HENRY

Agatha stood outside the open doorway of Henry's room resting her head against the wall, listening to Tippy talk about her dead brother, Leopold hanging hungrily on every word.

"We used to play all day, like, he'd even dress up. We'd get all fancy and he'd pretend to have this English accent—he was really good at it actually—and he'd wear this tuxedo with no shoes." Tippy paused, lost in a memory, and she lowered her eyes. "Henry hated wearing shoes."

Her words felt like a gut punch to Agatha. She wanted to tell Tippy about her imaginary friend and how he'd come to visit her years ago. But she was worried how Tippy would take the news and how weird it would make Agatha look or sound, not that she generally minded seeming weird. But this time felt different. She'd tell Tippy sometime, but that time certainly wasn't now.

Henry.

The fact that he'd been someone, a real, living, breathing, talking, existing thing chilled Agatha. "Henry," she repeated. And he'd been dead when he'd visited her. The heart within his body cold and still and yet he'd walked and talked and giggled and dreamed with her. Agatha couldn't believe it.

"There are times lately where I want to see or talk to him so bad, I can't stand it. Which is why I took that book," Tippy said, refashioning her bun with a multicolored scrunchie. "It's a bunch of garbage, though, like I said. Doesn't work."

"What exactly did you do?" Agatha said, appearing in the doorway. She felt she needed to know. There had to be a link between what Tippy had done and why Big was suddenly reappearing.

Tippy showed them her closet. "I sat in here with the candle and the book. I flipped around and did some sort of summoning spell, Chapter Four, I think? I can't remember. Anyway, nothing happened, and I blew out the candle and went to bed."

"That's it?" said Leopold.

"Yep." Tippy pulled a piece of gum from the pocket of her sweatpants. "Want some?" she said, holding it out, unbothered by the fact she'd tried to summon a dead boy a few days prior.

"No thanks," they both said simultaneously.

Tippy shrugged, heading for the door of her bedroom. "Well, better leave before my parents get home. I'm not allowed to really have visitors without them here. Especially boys." She eyed Leopold. "Girls are ok, though," she said and paused to smile at Agatha.

They descended the stairs, Agatha acutely aware it might be her last time on a circular stairwell.

"Thanks for the tour," Leopold said at the front door, grabbing his sneakers.

Agatha hesitated.

"What?" Tippy said, staring her up and down.

"Are you sure it didn't work?"

"Yeah. Nothing happened." Tippy answered hurriedly as Agatha stepped onto the porch, boots in hand, her right ankle crossed behind her left so Tippy wouldn't see her socks.

"Seriously, tell your Aunt I'm sorry," she said, shutting the door in Agatha's face.

CHAPTER 9
HELLO SISTER

Tippy leaned against the door and let out a breath. She was glad Agatha and Leopold had come by since she was ready to be rid of the book. After her attempt in the closet, things had seemed weird in the house. The air was strange, and it felt heavy, but Henry hadn't tried to contact her. She almost wished she hadn't done it. Almost.

"Good riddance," she muttered under her breath.

Tippy's cell phone chimed from the kitchen and she rushed to answer it.

"Honey," her mother's sweet voice spoke from the phone. "I'm going to be home late and so is dad. Maybe another hour or two. There's pizza in the freezer."

"It's fine, Mom." Tippy blew a bubble and popped it. Her parents were always late, working past closing time together at his law firm and now even on the weekends. "I'm not hungry anyway." She knew she'd have free reign over the television to watch some of her favorite murder shows.

"Ok, lovebug. Be home soon, and don't…." *Click*. The line was dead.

"Mom?"

The silence was replaced by a tone of repeated beeps, angry and forceful in her ear. Tippy hung up. "Don't what?" she said to herself, plopping herself down on one of the couches in the library. She selected a crime show on the television and pulled a fluffy purple blanket up to her shoulders.

The narrator's voice lulled her to sleep and somewhere in between wakefulness and dozing, Tippy heard footsteps. Close footsteps. She opened her eyes and peered around without moving. Dusk filled the room, painting the walls a sleepy grey, and the five o'clock traffic from Beach Boulevard hummed faintly in the background. She rubbed her eyes, noticing the television was off and the lights were out. She reached behind her for the lamp cord right behind the couch, sure that it was on when she fell asleep.

The click of the lamp's pull cord lit up the black screen of the silent television and Tippy immediately saw a reflection in it: something standing behind the couch. It darted quickly behind the heavy curtains, disappearing into the folds of the blue and white tapestry. Tippy sat up, her heart racing in her chest, her eyes still on the blank screen of the television. She couldn't bring herself to turn around. She kept her eyes on the curtains behind her, one lumpy fold in particular and inched her way off the couch to the floor.

She lay flat, peering under the couch toward the curtains behind it. Some dried cereal and a few pieces of popcorn blocked her view. Her breath sent the popcorn tumbling to the side like tumbleweeds she'd seen in coyote and roadrunner cartoons. Tippy could make out the bottom of the curtains, barely brushing the top of the white carpet and two dark feet peeking out from one of the folds. The toes were filthy and scrunched, as if gripping the carpet tightly either in anger or a desperate attempt to keep still. *Like an animal*, she thought.

But that wasn't all. Two dirty hands were on either side of the feet, as if the figure was crouching, and they too gripped the carpet angrily, the brownish nails digging into the white carpet. Tippy swallowed, feeling for her phone back on the couch, her left-hand gliding across the soft upholstery. She couldn't find it.

A low snarl from behind the curtain sent Tippy to her feet, running blindly toward the stairs without looking behind her. She heard nothing as she ran, skipping stairs in the rush to get to her room where she slammed the door behind her and pushed the lock on the knob. She stepped backwards toward her bed, keeping her eyes on the door. Her phone was still downstairs. What would she do now, she worried, gripping the wooden post of her bed until the tips of her fingers hurt.

Something paced outside her door, not on two feet, but on four, back and forth in an uneven tread indicating its intent to enter the room. Four dark fingers found their way to the gap under the door, scratching at the wood in a methodical way. Over and over and over again.

Tippy flung herself onto her bed and pulled her knees to her chest as a single tear dotted her cheek. "Stop!" she screamed. "Henry? Henry is that you? Stop it!" The scratching continued and she covered her ears, shaking her head violently until her dark hair fell from her bun in strands around her closed eyes. "Stoppppppp!" she wailed.

And suddenly it did.

Tippy reluctantly opened her eyes, keeping them squinted as she looked toward the door. Peering through her eyelashes, she saw one finger remaining under her door, frozen and pointing at something to her left. She turned her head slowly toward her nightstand, finding nothing out of place except her journal, which was deliberately opened to a clean, fresh, blank page. The white paper was stained and smudged with dirt, the writer apparently in a hurry.

Tippy leaned forward to see the sloppy writing, as a small little cry escaped her lips.

Hello sister

CHAPTER 10
THE DANCE PARTNER

On Sunday, it was Agatha's turn to cook dinner, a hurried concoction of boiled eggs, canned green beans and chicken tenders, which she and her mother ate quickly before getting ready for their second ballroom dancing lesson. To Agatha's disappointment, her mother hadn't given up. The weekend had been uneventful since Agatha's trip with Leopold to Tippy's. Agatha had decided not to return the book to Aunt Letty. She wanted to look through it herself, and strangely, Aunt Letty hadn't asked for it.

This particular evening, Sonny Anxious decided to have dinner with his sister Letty, whom he said seemed "off" in a whispered discussion Agatha overheard before dinner. Aunt Letty *always* seemed 'off.'

They arrived ten minutes late to the lesson, and Agatha hoped this meant her mother could be her partner, a dream that was immediately dashed when, upon entry, she saw only two gentlemen remained for grabs: her mother's partner from the last lesson and of course, Mr. Carr, who smiled warmly in Agatha's direction.

Anita Anxious took the outstretched hand of Mr. Burgess, giving her daughter a sheepish grin and a shrug, which Agatha returned with a glare before straightening her navy dress and half smiling at Mr. Carr. She took her place next to him, and they repeated their last week's lesson. He again took her hand in his, his grip cold and shaky. Agatha wasn't too upset, though, as she had questions.

She positioned her hand on his shoulder and looked down to avoid seeing the flipping and flopping of his unhinged tongue. "Where did you get the skull jar, Mr. Carr?"

"The what?"

"You know, the little jar you handed me last time?"

He paused as if trying to remember. "I found it. I think."

"How did you know it was for me?"

Mr. Carr seemed caught off guard by the question. He sniffled and reached for a handkerchief in his pocket. Old people were always carrying around handkerchiefs to catch phlegm and snot and all sorts of runny bodily liquids. The thought made Agatha want to gag.

"Huh," he started. "Well, I guess I don't know. It was a pretty jar. I thought maybe it was for you since you're pretty?"

Agatha smiled awkwardly knowing his comment meant no harm. "Yes, but you told me to be careful. Why did you say that?"

"Did I?"

"Yes."

"I don't know why I would've said that."

"Mr. Carr, I—"

"Ok, great job on that waltz, ladies and gentlemen! Great job!" The instructor interrupted, clapping her hands and praising her pupils. She took an extra second or two to aim several claps in Agatha's direction. Two or three other people clapped along.

"Why are they doing that? Clapping for me?" Agatha said aloud to Mr. Carr as the instructor shared a story about the history of the Cha-Cha.

"Perhaps they think you're good. You're a natural."

"Ok, but the skull jar," Agatha tried keeping him on subject.

"What jar?" Mr. Carr was sniffling again, and he dabbed his nose with the cream-colored handkerchief.

Agatha turned to face him. "What do you mean 'what jar?'"

Mr. Carr smiled sweetly, his loose tongue lolling around in the pockets of open flesh beneath his lower teeth. "I don't know. I just came here to dance, sweetie. I loved dancing when I was—"

Another set of loud claps from the instructor. "Ok. Focus up here. We've done the waltz. So, the Cha-Cha goes like this. It's just a sidestep, then rock, step, triple step, rock, step, triple step. Let me show you. I need a partner." She pretended to scan the room, immediately pointing at Agatha. "You, young lady. Let's get in some practice with a partner. Come up here."

Agatha felt the heat from her cheeks trickle to her neck as she trudged to the front of the room. The instructor clasped her hands, her seventy-five gold bracelets jiggling loudly around her slender wrists. She smelled of gardenias and roses and every other flower under the sun, and the mingled scents threatened Agatha with a headache. The instructor gripped her close, aggressively, but the lady was warm, unlike Mr. Carr.

"Like this!" she shouted and moved Agatha with her as she did the dance number. "And one, two, three and cha-cha! One, and two, three and cha-cha, one!" Agatha tried to keep up. It was a relatively easy dance, requiring regular steps and then three quick steps in a row. "Wonderful, young lady. I am so impressed," the instructor said when they were finished, and she motioned for Agatha to return to the spot where she was before. Agatha obliged, happy to be removed from the spotlight.

"Ok, now your turn!" she yelled to her crowd of dance students. "And one, two, three, and cha-cha!"

Her voice became a lull in Agatha's head as she rejoined Mr. Carr. She opened her mouth to again ask about the jar but changed her mind. His cold hand gently took hers as they tried the cha-cha for the next fifteen minutes in silence, a smile on his face and his gaze faraway as if he wasn't aware of Agatha's presence.

"Wonderful, wonderful!" The instructor's voice broke Agatha's thoughts. "Try to practice at home this week everyone!"

"Goodnight, Mr. Carr," Agatha said, not meeting his eyes and gathering her purse, which she slung over one shoulder. She hurried past him to the door before he could respond, joining her mother in the car. The station wagon swallowed Anita Anxious in the driver's seat, her messy bun and large brown glasses giving her an exaggerated appearance.

"Honey, I just can't even tell you how good you are," she said, putting the vehicle in reverse and pulling out of the parking lot. "So, so proud of you. You're a natural."

"Why does everybody keep saying that? What are you talking about?"

"Your dancing. I mean the steps aren't hard, but it just takes a lot of courage to dance like that, you know."

Agatha peered out the window at the horizon. The beach was dark, the sun having set long ago. Several lights dotted the shore, families with flashlights looking for sand crabs. *Visitors*, Agatha thought. *Nobody gets in the beach water*.

Her thoughts suddenly snagged on her mother's words. "Courage? To dance like what?"

Anita yanked at her bun, the rubber band getting tangled in a clump of blonde hair. "You know, honey. Alone."

Agatha scrunched her face. "What do you mean alone? When?"

Her mother nodded. "Last week and tonight."

"What?"

"Oh, don't get flustered," her mother said, one hand on the steering wheel and the other still working the knot in her hair. "I'm just saying it is brave of you to be the only person without a partner and still doing the dance moves."

"Mom, what are you talking about? My partner is Mr. Carr."

Anita Anxious' hand froze in her hair, and she let out a nervous giggle. "That's not funny," she said.

"Yeah, well I don't think it is either. I have to look at his tongue wiggling all over the place while he's trying to talk to me. I mean he's always been nice, but his hands are super cold, and the mouth thing is just so—"

"Agatha!" her mother cut her off. "You stop that right now. I mean it."

"I didn't say anything bad, mom!" she protested. "I just mean it's kinda creepy to have to hold his hand and stuff." She turned to her mother who kept her eyes on the road. Agatha saw a small, plump little tear form in the corner of her eye. "Mom? What's wrong?"

"Agatha," her mother sniffled, putting her hand to her mouth to keep from crying, giving up on the knotted hair which fell to the side of her head. "Oh, honey..."

"Mom? What?

Anita Anxious kept her eyes on the road ahead, her bottom lip quivering until she found the words. "Mr. Carr died last month."

CHAPTER 11
UNDER THE COVERS

Agatha stormed into her room after the car ride home with her mother and plopped herself down inside her closet. She shut the door and put her head in her hands. The amount of convincing she'd had to do on the way home, coupled with numerous apologies, making sure her mother thought she'd been joking. *No, Mom, I was kidding. Yes, I promise. No, Mom, I didn't really see Mr. Carr. Yes, Mom I was being a jerk making fun of Mr. Carr like that. Yes, Mom, I was dancing alone all this time looking like a crazy person in front of all those people. MAYBE I AM CRAZY!*

Mr. Carr had been dead this entire time, and she hadn't noticed? Of course he'd been dead. He's the one who handed her the skull jar. Wasn't Mr. Dominicus the one, in a roundabout way with Aunt Hattie present, who'd found the first skull jar? And he was dead too! Agatha nibbled the side of her thumb and picked at its cuticle. Mr. Carr seemed very confused this evening, and she wondered if he even knew he was dead. Perhaps he was content just floating around dancing, no worries in the world, happy with his far off glassy-eyed look.

Agatha pulled her dress up over her head and kicked off her shoes. She chose one of her dad's old t-shirts from a sloppy stack in her closet, and it swallowed her little body in one gulp. Settling herself in between several mismatched sheets and blankets which covered her bed, Agatha rubbed a knuckle against her teeth while thinking, trying hard not to put the finger in her mouth.

The reality of what her mother said in the car hit her again, and it was frightening. Mr. Carr was dead. All these dead people everywhere, all the time. Some needed help. Some needed no help. Some refusing help. Isn't that what Aunt Hattie had said? Blanche Caillavet was the one ghost she couldn't help. Why?

"Agatha?" her father waved his hand in the open crack of the doorway. That was his way of giving his daughter privacy and asking for permission to enter, waving just his hand in the crack of the door.

"Yes."

He poked his head through and smiled. "Hi. Mind if I sit?" He entered, carrying HattieCat who was nudging him on his neck. He placed her on Agatha's bed where she curled up near the pillows, staring at Sonny Anxious. *If Dad only knew,* Agatha thought sadly.

Her father sat at her desk, and Macbeth, the family's German Shepherd, followed him in, pacing a few times before deciding to join Agatha on her bed, too. HattieCat hissed disapprovingly at the dog but made no move to leave and continued her wide-eyed interest in the conversation.

"You saw Aunt Letty yesterday, right?" He said, jiggling the cup of Scrabble pieces in his hands, picking through the tiles with his head down.

"Yes. Why?"

"I just had dinner with her. She seemed worried about something but told me everything was fine."

Agatha didn't respond. She wanted to ask if they'd eaten at a restaurant or if he'd gone to Aunt Hattie's old house for dinner, but she already knew the answer. Aunt Letty didn't like going out. She rubbed Macbeth's ears instead, and he willingly gave her his tummy, begging for more.

"Did she say anything to you?"

"No? But I don't think she'd say anything to me anyway, Dad. She's kind of..." Agatha searched for appropriate word. "...mysterious?" She didn't want to tell him about Tippy and the book.

Sonny Anxious shook his head, his head full of black curls wiggling about his face. He needed a haircut, Agatha thought.

"I guess she is," he said finally. "I guess she's just as upset as the rest of us about the loss of...Hattie." The pause in his sentence was an eternity. "Anyway, what are you thinking of your new cousin?" He was changing the subject.

"Well, he's not new is he?"

Her father smiled. "I guess not."

"Dad, how long have you known about Tobie?"

Sonny Anxious looked confused. "What do you mean? Since the day he was born of course. We even told you about him when you were younger, not that you'd remember. And since all those years passed without seeing Letty or her son, I guess it wasn't a topic of conversation. But yes, Hattie..." he paused again. "...called and told me about his birth."

Agatha sat up. "She was there?"

He shook his head. "Yes. She went and stayed with Letty for quite a few months, to help her."

This was news to Agatha. She didn't know that her two aunts had been that close, but then again, she really wouldn't know, would she? With Aunt Letty never being around and all.

Agatha was in a prodding mood. "Why did Aunt Letty leave the Coast in the first place?"

The question seemed unexpected to Sonny Anxious, and he leaned back in the chair, interlacing his hands behind his head. He opened his mouth to say something then paused. "You know, I'll be honest, Agatha. I really don't know. She said she had a better job opportunity in Texas, but I always felt it was something more, possibly even something to do with Harriet."

Agatha had never had such an open conversation with her father, and she couldn't decide whether she was uncomfortable or wanted to prod more. Aunt Hattie was possibly the reason Aunt Letty left the Coast? Another mystery to unravel. Her family was one big ball of yarn, intertwined and knotted with a myriad of half-truths, puzzles, riddles and secrets.

"I hadn't seen her until I asked her to come run Hattie's shop. Maybe she's always been odd." He thought for a moment, standing up. "Or maybe she's just being herself and I'm not used to it. I don't know." He grabbed Agatha's knee under the blanket with a smile. "Well, goodnight."

"Goodnight, Dad." She turned off her light and snuggled into bed next to HattieCat, confused as ever. Her face touched the cat's cold, wet nose, and her thoughts drifted to Mr. Carr. His touch had been cold too, as cold as Big's. "What are you and Aunt Letty hiding, Auntie?" she asked the cat as her eyelids grew heavy.

Moments or minutes or hours passed—Agatha couldn't distinguish which—before a sound awakened her.

Tap.

The sound had been so low, at first, she ignored it.

Tap.

Agatha sat up and looked around. Where was HattieCat? Had she gotten out?

Tap tap. It was coming from her window. Leopold?

Her toes touched the floor, and she made her way to the window, her fingers snaking their way in between the slats of the blinds. Her backyard was empty. She let her gaze drift to the fence and beyond, but all was quiet in the cemetery, too. Even her mother's windchimes were silent. Maybe it was something invisible? Agatha tapped her window twice but got no response.

She yawned. "You'll have to do more than tap, then," she said aloud, finding the warmth of her sheets again. Macbeth lay in a heap now at the end of her bed, having made himself comfortable under the covers. "Goodnight, buddy," she whispered.

She lay on her stomach and faced her window, the blinds still partially open, waiting for the tapping again. Deciding to be brave, she let her arm fall over the side of the bed in the darkness, something she never did. An exposed foot or dangling arm while sleeping freaked her out, and she usually covered herself in blankets all the way up to her ears, as if they provided some sort of armor against the things that lurk in the night.

Her fingers brushed against her sheets and the bed rail until they fell on something soft and warm. She snatched her hand back, immediately recognizing what she'd touched. *Macbeth.* She sat up, pressing her head against her headboard, not wanting to look at her feet.

If Macbeth was on the floor by her bed, what was the lump under her blankets?

Her shaking fingers reached for a small flashlight she kept on her nightstand. She peeled back the first layer of sheets and clicked the flashlight button. She shone the light toward her feet and as she suspected, the light fell on a mass of orange curly hair which revealed a face and round circular eyes in an expression of torment. Big clamped his hand around Agatha's foot, digging his little nails into her ankle, and she screamed.

CHAPTER 12
DOOM'S MASKERADES

Agatha awoke on the couch. She'd scrambled there in terror the night before, Macbeth in tow, telling her parents not to worry about the scream as she'd only had a nightmare. She was finding her interactions with her parents lately were filled with lies.

The sounds and smells of bacon and sausage wafted from the kitchen, the sizzling of grease in the pan. The toaster popped with finished bread, and she heard her mother humming. *Breakfast*.

"Mom?" she said, groggily, pouring herself some water from the kitchen sink. "Don't you have to work today?"

"No, honey. Penny took the shift for me." Anita Anxious expertly flipped two eggs in the pan without breaking the yolks. Her mother was making those for herself, she knew, because Agatha hated runny eggs.

"Oh, and I might have her over sometime this week for a game night. She's really fun. Remember I trained her a few months ago? I think she has a kid your age she could bring."

"Uh-huh," Agatha slid into one of the brown wooden chairs around the table. HattieCat followed, winding herself between her ankles and mewing. "Is it a boy or a girl?"

"Who?"

"Your coworker's kid. Is it a boy or a girl?" These were important questions. Agatha was far more comfortable with boys. Her interactions with girls as of late had been few and far between, and generally she avoided them, if possible, not liking the squirmy feelings they gave her. Most were either judgy or obnoxious or far too popular to be friends with anyway, Tippy among the latter. Agatha didn't want or need many friends.

Her mother set a plate of scrambled eggs and sausage links in front of her. "I think a boy? Maybe not." She shrugged. "I've got to run a couple errands this morning, and you're going to go with me." She pinched Agatha's cheek as she returned to the kitchen.

Agatha didn't protest. "Where are we going?"

"Well since tomorrow is Mardi Gras, I've got to run by that mask shop in Vieux Marche."

Agatha froze, a flimsy piece of egg dangling from her bottom lip. It hit her plate with a splat. "What for?"

"Well, Mardi Gras stuff, of course, honey. I know you hate the parades, but the restaurant has their usual float, and I'm riding in it. You don't have to come tomorrow, but I wish you would." She gave Agatha a pouty face, and Agatha rolled her eyes.

"Maybe. I don't like crowds."

"I know," Anita Anxious slurped her coffee thoughtfully. "That mask shop has some pretty stuff though, and I've got a coupon too.

Maybe you'll find something you want."

Definitely not, Agatha thought to herself, not wanting to bring a single thing home from that place. Her thoughts drifted to Dorian Doom, and she wondered if he would be working today since they had no school. Her stomach rumbled with nervousness. She wolfed down two sausage links and excused herself from the table. She hurried to her bedroom in search of her most flattering grey dress and frowned to find it in her dirty clothes hamper. But it passed the sniff test, so over her head it went.

The Golden Fisherman statue still stood guard over Vieux Marche like some tyrant requiring a toll before shoppers could visit the stores lining the small street.

"I know you hate that thing," her mother said, seeing her face. "It really is very ugly."

Agatha shook her head and apprehensively followed her mother into Doom's Maskerades. The last time she'd set foot in the shop, she'd encountered what she considered to be old, awakened evil. Once inside, she gasped.

The store inside was nothing like what she remembered. No mirrors lining the walls, nor creaky wooden floor. No dark cases on either side of the aisle. Instead, Agatha was met with a happier, more cheerful storefront. Beige carpet, clear glass cases lined with brass, white walls, and decorations all the colors indicative of Mardi Gras: gold, green and purple. And there, behind the cash register was another thing Agatha was surprised, yet pleased, to see: Dorian Doom. She looked away.

"I'm going to look around in the back," she heard her mother say, heading to the back room which was no longer closed off by a black velvet curtain. It appeared to be the room where they sold the masks, and Agatha shuddered.

"You know, the last time you were here, there was a mess so big my father thought someone broke in." Dorian was beside her now, a baseball cap smushing his dark brown hair against his forehead and casting a shadow over his already mysterious face.

Agatha smirked. “A lot has changed.”

Dorian looked around. “My dad thought it was time, I guess. Not as gloomy.”

“I like gloomy,” Agatha said, thoughtfully.

“I don’t,” he said, nodding toward the back room of the store where Agatha’s mother was picking out several masks.

“Oh.” Agatha knew exactly what he meant. “I’m guessing you haven’t seen the ghost again?”

Dorian stared at her, his blue eyes meeting hers before darting away. “So, what are you doing for Mardi Gras?” he asked, unenthusiastically. He straightened a few of the objects on the wall, his back to her.

“I hate Mardi—” She was interrupted by two more people who entered the store, one of which was none other than Tippy Trinkle.

Agatha started to wave but dropped her hand. Tippy looked terrible, like she hadn’t slept in days. Dark circles framed her eyes, and her hair was a knotted mess. Her cheeks were puffy like she’d been crying, and her backpack sloppily dangled off her shoulders. Her left fist gripped a wad of crumpled cash, and she looked down, as if she was embarrassed to find Agatha at the store.

“Oh, hey Tippy,” Dorian said. “I have your mom’s order ready. Be right back.” He disappeared down the aisle to one of the cases, being careful not to step anywhere near the opening to the back room.

Tippy stood near Agatha but kept her eyes on her shoes. An entire planet of awkwardness revolved and rotated around them both before Dorian returned with a small bag. Tippy thrust the cash at him, dropping some of the bills on the counter and rushed out the door.

Dorian shrugged. “Well, ok then.” He counted out a twenty dollar bill and several one dollar bills in front of Agatha. "She looked bad, didn't she?"

Agatha saw her mother paying at the cash register, a large bag of beads and trinkets in tow, and she knew her time with Dorian was ending. She decided to be bold. "The ghost," she said to Dorian, "The one in the back room. Did you ever see her again?"

Dorian stopped counting the money. "No..." his sentence seemed unfinished, as if he had more to say, but decided against it.

"Are you sure?"

"Are you Mr. Doom's son?" Agatha's mother joined them, holding out her hand to shake Dorian's.

"Yes, ma'am. I'm Dorian."

"So nice to meet you. Do you and Agatha have any classes together?"

Dorian scratched his head, as uncomfortable with small talk as Agatha. "Yes ma'am, a couple." He pointed to her large bags. "Can I help you outside with those?"

Anita Anxious smiled big. "Well, sure! That would be lovely. Actually, Agatha," she turned to her daughter, handing her the car keys. "I'm going to get one more bag of beads. Open the wagon for Dorian, will you?"

Agatha flinched at the word 'wagon.'

Dorian loaded the bags in the trunk of the car, and Anita Anxious joined them a few moments later, plopping herself behind the steering wheel. Agatha nodded to Dorian who went back into the shop.

"Here," her mother said, handing her two dollars.

"What's this for?"

She pointed toward the mask shop. "Go give that to Dorian. It's a tip."

Agatha scrunched her face. “Do I have to?”

“Of course, you do, dear. Now go on,” Anita Anxious gently nudged her daughter.

Yanking open the door to the shop, Agatha found Dorian hanging up another mask. “Here,” she said. “From my mom.”

“Thanks.” Dorian tucked the money in the back pocket of his jeans. He removed his ballcap and fluffed his hair before smashing it back down on his head again. “And uh, you let her out.” “What?” “To answer your question. No, I haven’t seen the ghost again. And you should know why that is.”

Agatha did know, sort of, and didn’t want to hear it. Aunt Hattie was right when she said she didn’t want to speak things out loud for fear of them coming true. Agatha didn’t want to hear Dorian say it, so she nodded, hoping that was enough.

It wasn’t.

Dorian’s eyes were serious and sad at the same time. “I haven’t seen the ghost again after that night because YOU let her out.”

CHAPTER 13
THE SHADOW

Tippy set the bag from Doom's Maskerades in the basket on her bike and pedaled slowly toward home. She'd been all too happy to run an errand for her mother and escape the walls of her humongous house which lately felt like a prison. The last two days had been an endless cycle of growls in dark places like closets and under her bed, weird, childlike giggles in the night, and footsteps pacing all night outside her door. And then last night, in the middle of the one hour of sleep she managed to get, she awoke to find a shadow standing at the foot of her bed, smiling. When their eyes met, it held up a dirty hand and waved. Agatha now had the book, and Tippy wondered if there was a spell in there for UN-doing what she'd done. Now all she wanted now was for her brother to *go away*.

Besides her quick errand to the mask shop, Tippy had a plan. She reached Irish Hill Drive, and though she never usually cut through the cemetery, today was different. Henry was buried there, and she wanted to try something. She was desperate. Her bike screeched to a halt in front of one of the roads leading in and she looked around.

Nobody.

Her heart pounded against her ribs, in her neck and through her ears as she steered the bike toward the front corner where Henry was buried. Several old oaks leaned over their family plot like a canopy, making his grave shaded and dark. Most of the graves in the front part of the cemetery were a couple hundred years old, indicative of how long the Trinkle family had been in Biloxi.

Her handlebars hit the grass and she faced his headstone, tidy because of her mother. This was Tippy's first visit to his grave since he'd died.

She sat on the grass with her bag, producing the candle she'd conveniently not given back to Agatha a couple days prior. The February day offered no breeze, and the flame eagerly attached itself to the wick. She no longer had the book, but perhaps she could just talk her way out of her problem. Maybe her brother could hear her. After all, his body was lying six feet beneath her.

Chills hit her neck, and she scooted to the side of the grave. "Um," she said, her voice breaking. "Henry?"

The cars roared by on Beach Boulevard, no one concerned with a young girl sitting in the cemetery speaking to her dead sibling.

"You're scaring me, and I—" she hesitated. "I need you to leave. Like, leave me alone."

Silence was the response, as she'd expected, but she continued. "I wanted to see you, but you're not yourself and I shouldn't have done what I did. I need you to go away."

The iron gate at the front entrance to the cemetery suddenly swung open a few inches with a loud creak and Tippy stood up. No one was there. Chills peppered her body as if hyper aware of something being amiss and altogether wrong.

"Please. Please just go away." She blew out the candle and hurried to stuff it back in her bag as the gate creaked closed and back open again.

Snap.

A branch above her moved and several leaves fell to the ground, but Tippy paid no attention. Her eyes were on the gate. A low snicker caused her to look upwards, and she saw him wedged between two large arms of an oak tree. Her mouth fell open in terror.

The silhouette arched its back, and Tippy could still make out every last detail of what was once her brother. His long eyelashes and arched eyebrows, the curls of his hair that moved as he breathed, and the curves of his cheeks which began beside his wild eyes and ended at his lips in a wicked smile.

The shadow crouched in the tree, his tuxedo dirty at the cuffs. It rocked back and forth in between the two limbs, as if preparing to leap, and Tippy turned to run. She thought she saw the figure move in her periphery, and she tripped over her bicycle, landing sprawled on her back. Her brother was still in her view, and she saw he hadn't left the tree. Instead, he smiled again, angrier and more wicked than before. He raised a lone finger, blackened by dirt and death, and moved it back and forth as if to reprimand her.

Henry scaled the tree's trunk using his hands and feet as claws and crawled directly over Tippy, though he didn't touch her. A heaviness settled into her chest and stomach, and her limbs pressed into the ground beneath her. He leaned to her ear, his putrid breath coming to rest under her nose, and he spoke in a voice that was not her brother's, his words forming a promise which paralyzed her.

"I'm not going anywhere."

CHAPTER 14
PUT HIM BACK

Agatha was on edge. She gnawed a knuckle while pacing her bedroom, every now and then eyeing the skull jar she'd received from Mr. Carr. It sat, unassuming, on a shelf by the other one, but there was nothing sweet or innocent about either. Agatha glanced over to her bed where HattieCat was curled up on one of the pillows. She eyed the cat suspiciously, narrowing her eyes at it, but the cat paid no attention.

And Tippy. She'd never seen Tippy like that before. Tippy was always well put together, with a face full of designer makeup, freshly painted nails, and the nicest clothes, the likes of which the Anxious family could never afford. Even her messiest bun was a perfect one, like Agatha had witnessed the other day.

But today was different. Her sloppy appearance indicated something more than just a couple nights of bad sleep. There was something lurking beneath the surface, something only someone like Agatha Anxious could see. A combination of fear, worry, and dread she'd seen before. It reminded her of the older picture of Blanche Caillavet she'd ripped from the library book the night she and Leopold broke into the mask shop and encountered the old, angry ghost. Today, Tippy had the same look.

Agatha stretched her back and yawned, kneeling next to the side of the bed where HattieCat lay. She placed a hand on the cat's tail, running her fingers down to the tip and leaned in.

"Aunt Hattie?" she whispered. "Are you there?"

HattieCat headbutted Agatha's hand and mewed but said no more, resting her head back on the pillow.

Agatha checked her watch. It was only seven. No bumps in the covers tonight didn't mean she wouldn't be surprised by Big. He was everywhere at any moment in time. Agatha curled up next to HattieCat and buried a hand in the warm fur of her tummy.

"I miss you, Auntie," she said, watching the rise and fall of HattieCat's chest until her own eyelids began to close, the cat's gentle purring soothing her to sleep.

Agatha awoke in an upright position on the living room couch, her small feet dangling over the edge. Her hand was still on HattieCat, and the room was dark.

Did I sleepwalk?

"Mom!" she yelled, her voice echoing off the four walls of the small room. As her eyes adjusted to the darkness, she became aware of a figure standing in the opening of the hallway, facing her, its thin lanky body leaning against the doorframe.

"Mom?" It was too tall to be her mother, and too thin to be her father. She squinted to see more of the silhouette and just as her eyes recognized the outline, it was upon her. With the quickness of rushing water, the figure came barreling toward her until it touched her hair with its finger, placing a piece of it behind her ear.

Lucius Nikolai.

Agatha started to scream but couldn't, and suddenly, nothing on her body worked. Her legs and arms were frozen, her face felt numb, and she couldn't turn her head to avoid looking into his reptilian eyes, which blinked with two sets of eyelids.

Nikolai smiled, partially exposing his hundreds of teeth and black gums. "Have you seen the darkness yet, Agatha?"

Her voice was thick-tongued and sluggish, like she was speaking in slow motion. "How...did...youuuu..." Drool spilled from the side of her mouth and her lips drooped.

"Shhhh," he placed a finger to his lips, and backed away. "You must find the light."

Tap!

A rock hit her window and Agatha sat up abruptly in a panic. Sweat pooled where her body had been, and her t-shirt was soaked. She recognized the walls of her bedroom.

A dream.

Knock!

Agatha threw off her covers to make sure Big wasn't at her feet, but her bed was empty.

Knock! Knock! Knock! A group of pebbles hit the glass windowpane simultaneously. Someone was at her window for real this time. Agatha yanked open her blinds and stared into the same dark eyed puffy face from earlier. Tippy Trinkle was standing in her backyard. Agatha unlocked and opened the window, and Tippy climbed through without being invited, landing with a thud on Agatha's floor. Both girls froze momentarily to see if Agatha's parents would be coming down the hallway. Silence. Agatha pulled down her blinds and flipped on a small shell-shaped nightlight.

Tippy was gasping, trying to whisper an entire story in one breath, and she spoke in a desperate whisper. "He's here! I guess it did work, Agatha! And now I don't know what to do but he won't leave me alone and he's everywhere. He's at home, he's in the cemetery, he's anywhere I am all the time and he's mean. Oh my gosh he's really mean and not himself. I don't understand! It's him, it's HIM, Agatha! How do I make him go away? Please make him to go awayyyyyy!" She fell back into a pile on Agatha's floor, weeping.

Agatha sat back against her closet door, watching Tippy's body heave with sobs. She wasn't sure what to say and let Tippy have a few moments to cry. After a while, Tippy collected herself. "Can I sit at your desk?" She pointed toward the chair, wiping her nose with the sleeve of her sweatshirt.

Agatha remained on the floor. "Sure."

Tippy stared at the Scrabble board. "I only saw two windows at the back of your house, and I knew one of them had to be yours. I got lucky on the first try," she sniffled.

"Tippy—" Agatha started.

"It...worked." Tippy swallowed and laid her head on the desk. "I keep seeing him. And I just want him to go away now because he's different."

"Big?" The word left Agatha's lips, and she caught herself, cupping her hand over her mouth.

Tippy's head shot up. "How do you know that name?"

Agatha's hand remained over her mouth as she decided what to say. "I was scared to tell you because I thought you wouldn't believe me." She cleared her throat, swallowing a little gurgle of loosened phlegm before continuing. "About five years ago, I had an imaginary friend. I was the only one who could see him. He rarely said anything, and we just sort of played, you know, jump rope or tea or climbing trees or whatever. He had the brightest orange hair I'd ever seen, and it was curly. And a gap—"

"Between his front teeth," Tippy finished.

"Yes. And sometimes he whispered things in an English accent. He said his name was Big, and one day he was just gone." Agatha pulled her knees up to her chest, covering them with her t-shirt. "I didn't know he was dead until now. To me, he was real."

"He *was* real." Tippy stared at the skull jars on Agatha's shelf. "My parents called him Big as a nickname because he wasn't at all. He was very small—well, I guess we both were—and the nickname was just for fun. I was Pig because I ate a lot, I guess. Big and Pig." Her bottom lip quivered.

Agatha folded her hands in her lap. "I never saw him again until recently, and I didn't know his real name until I saw the picture at your house."

"So, you've seen him too? I mean, lately? Is he mean?"

Agatha shook her head. "No, Big isn't mean to me, but he's not the same. He's..." she searched for the word. "Frightened, maybe? Like he needs help or something."

"Why would he visit you? And why did he visit you five years ago? That would have been right after he died." Tippy wiped away a small tear with the back of her hand.

Agatha was too tired to explain all that came with being a Perceiver, so she kept it simple. "I can see ghosts and help them. I know that probably sounds ridiculous, but I guess Big needs something now and maybe he needed something years ago too, but I didn't know since I was so young." She looked away from Tippy, embarrassed.

Tippy sighed. "Maybe he's mad with me for waking him up or whatever you want to call it. Do you know how to make him go away?"

"When ghosts come to me, they usually need like, help or something. When they get what they need, they disappear. Like, after I help them, I don't see them again, I mean." Agatha stood and opened her closet, feeling the top shelf while on her tippy toes.

"Has he told you what he needs help with? He doesn't talk to me like that. He just..." Tippy frowned. "...he just snarls and growls and stuff and like, threatens me." She put her head in her hands.

"No, he doesn't talk to me."

"I thought you said he asked for help?" said Tippy.

"He mouthed it, but he doesn't speak." Agatha cocked her head to the side and paused. "Huh. The last ghost I helped didn't speak either, until I helped him get his coin back. Maybe that's a thing? Maybe they don't speak until I help them." *Or maybe they can't*...she thought.

"Well, what do we do?" Tippy sniffled again.

Agatha's fingers finally found what she was looking for: Aunt Letty's book. She threw it on the bed where it landed face up with a thud.

"If this is what brought him here, then I'm guessing this is what will put him back."

CHAPTER 15

THE NEWEST ASSIGNMENT

Agatha sat on her bed and opened the book. "It was Chapter Four," Tippy said impatiently, joining Agatha amongst the pillows and settling in like they'd been friends for years. She smelled of vanilla and cream, and Agatha felt envious for a fleeting moment.

"Ok, but let me just see what's before Chapter Four," Agatha said, thumbing through the book.

"Why?" asked Tippy.

"Did you not read anything before Chapter Four?"

"No." Tippy searched for an excuse. "I was in a hurry."

Now I see why we have this problem, Agatha thought. She flipped to the table of contents and ran her fingers down the list, reading the chapters aloud. "Chapter One: Introduction. Chapter Two: The Importance of Purpose. Chapter Three: Items Necessary for Summoning. Chapter Four: The Act of Summoning. Chapter Five: Reversing the Spell..."

"That's it!" Tippy shouted.

"Shhhh!" Agatha whispered.

"Sorry, sorry. That's it. What's that chapter say, the reversing the spell one?"

"Hold on," Agatha was still reading. "Chapter Six: If Nothing Happens. And Chapter Seven: Life After Summoning." Agatha flipped through the last few pages of the book and saw an epilogue entitled "A Note on Deceivers." *Why was that word familiar?*

"Agatha!" Tippy's whisper was excited and rushed. She grabbed the book from Agatha's hands. "I'm telling you, what we need is Chapter five." She flipped to the middle of the book until she came to the chapter. "Here," she thrust the book back into Agatha's hands. "I'm sure you read quicker than me."

Agatha skimmed through until she found what she was looking for. She scrunched her face. "No way."

"What?" said Tippy.

Agatha paused. "It says that a spirit can be summoned from anywhere, but to put a spirit back, you must go to where the death occurred."

Tippy's mouth dropped open.

Agatha gulped. "We have to go to the place he died."

Tippy closed her mouth. "Read it to me."

"It says," Agatha began. "If at any point after summoning, your purpose has been fulfilled or the object of your summoning, hereafter called a summonee, requires resituating (which is defined as sending the summonee back to its rightful realm)—" Agatha stopped. "Realm? What's that mean?"

Tippy shushed her. "Keep reading!"

"Ok, ok." Agatha started over. "If at any point after summoning, your purpose has been fulfilled or the object of your summoning, hereafter called a summonee, requires resituating, (which is defined as sending the summonee back to its rightful realm), it is necessary to return to the place where the summonee originally left the earth. Once there, the same exact steps should be taken with the same exact items as when originally performing the summoning spell, with the exception that wording will be different. The summoner this time shall say the summonee's name, date of death, and 'I return you to sleep' thrice."

"Thrice?" Tippy said.

Agatha looked up at her. "Three times."

"Oh, yes. Ok."

Agatha closed the book softly, her mind elsewhere. She'd heard stories over the years about the Back Bay Hospital. It had been closed and abandoned for a few years, completely trashed, and recently had become the spooky spot for local teenagers who wished to measure their courage by staying the night there.

The hospital also had a reputation for housing ghosts. Indeed, it had a morgue, and a great number of Gulf Coasters had died there, but one local story stood out. Something to do with twins haunting the place, but Agatha didn't know much more than that. She'd never been to the hospital, and her mother didn't believe in ghosts, so tales like that weren't told around the Anxious family home. It was a story Aunt Hattie used to try to spook her with over popcorn and black and white creepy movies. Now Agatha wondered if the 'ghost twin' was Henry.

"It's not too far from here," Tippy said, breaking up her thoughts.

Agatha nodded. "But it's too late tonight, and tomorrow is Mardi Gras. Too many people and parades." She paused. "Wait maybe that's not a bad thing. Do you have a phone?"

"A cell phone? Yeah," said Tippy, producing one from the pocket of her sweatshirt.

"Like, with internet and stuff?"

Tippy puckered her lips. "Whose cell phone doesn't have internet?"

Agatha's cheeks flushed. "Can I see yours?"

Tippy tossed it to her. Without looking, Agatha figured it to be the newest, most updated cell phone offered on the market, but much to her surprise, her eyes rested upon an old phone, very much like hers.

Tippy read Agatha's look of surprise with expert skill. "I told ya. Just because my parents have money doesn't mean I do."

Still, Agatha thought. *At least she has internet.*

Tippy was putting her long, black hair into a ponytail. "What are you looking for?"

"I'm looking up the parade routes for tomorrow night. If there's one right near the hospital, even better. We'd have a reason to be close, and no one will be paying attention." After a few moments of scrolling, she said, "Found it. Well, close enough." She handed the phone back to Tippy. "The Krewe of Jupiter parade is just a few streets over. Lots of people are around, but no one will be noticing what we're doing. It starts at 6:30. We can go to the parade and head to the hospital once it's dark."

"Dark?" Tippy shivered.

"If it's daytime, someone would probably see us. What will you tell your parents?"

Tippy shrugged. "Nothing. My parents work a lot. They don't care."

"Oh. Well, what about tonight?"

She shook her head emphatically. "I can't go home. Not while it's dark, at least. Henry is probably waiting for me. Can I maybe sleep on your floor and climb out of the window in the morning?"

Agatha smiled. It reminded her of the time, not too long ago, when she slept in Leopold's carport. That was the same evening she discovered who Mr. Dominicus really was. "Sure," she said. "But you gotta be gone by six. My mom gets up then."

"Thanks."

Another thought crossed Agatha's mind. "I've got to make a phone call." She checked the time. It was nearly midnight. She tiptoed to the kitchen where her cell phone was lying on the counter and texted Leopold.

Agatha: *Are you up?*

Leopold: *Hi.*

Agatha: *Hi.*

Leopold: *Hi.*

Agatha: *Stop being weird. New mission. Tomorrow night. Krewe of Jupiter parade. Meet at your house at 6pm. Deets later.* (She'd recently heard this abbreviated word for 'details' and couldn't wait to use it sometime. Now seemed like the perfect opportunity.)

Leopold: *New ghost?*

Agatha: *Fill you in then. Deets later.* (Too much to use it twice?)

Leopold: . . .

Agatha: *Go to bed.*

Leopold: *No. Now.*

Agatha: *What? The deets?* (Ok, now this was excessive and no longer cool whatsoever. She wished she could delete a text.)

Leopold: *Tell me now.*

Agatha: *Fine. Can you come to my window? Four knocks. My nightlight is on.*

Leopold: *Nightlight? Scared of the dark, Agatha Anxious?*

Agatha set her phone back on the counter face down in the same position it had been. Her parents' one rule was the phone had to be on the counter and charging after 9:30, so she wasn't allowed to call or send texts after that time. Agatha didn't really mind. She didn't have many—or any—friends she needed to talk to late in the evening. Except of course Leopold.

When she returned to her room, Tippy had taken two pillows and one blanket off the bed and made herself a palette on the floor. "Is that ok?" she asked Agatha when she reappeared in the doorway.

"Sure," Agatha said.

"Who'd you have to call?"

"I texted Leopold."

Tippy sat up. "Panic? Leopold Panic? What for?"

"He helps me with all my stuff. He can see things too."

Tippy looked confused. "Are y'all a thing?"

Agatha wasn't sure what Tippy was insinuating but it sounded gross. "Just friends."

"He can see ghosts too?" Tippy stretched out on the blankets and fluffed one of the pillows as if she'd been to countless sleepovers at Agatha's house.

Tap.Tap.

Agatha rolled her eyes. "Yes, he can. But he obviously doesn't follow directions. Or maybe he can't count," she said, lifting the blinds. "I said knock four times, Leop—"

Agatha stopped at the window. Tippy noticed.

"What's wrong?"

Agatha didn't answer. Instead, she watched Big take a seat on one of the rusty swings in her backyard. He gently pushed off from the ground, the swing moving ever so slightly as if weighted down by nothing more than a feather. He stared at Agatha and frowned, his eyebrows smushed together in pain.

"Is it Leopold?" Tippy said, joining Agatha at the window.

Big dug a toe into the dirt and abruptly stopped the swing, staring at the girl who stood next to Agatha. His lips parted in surprise. He turned and ran toward the cemetery, his ghostly body passing right through the backyard fence.

Tippy backed away from the window. "I don't want to see him! He's come for me, hasn't he?"

Big continued to run toward the front of the cemetery, his orange curls bouncing atop his head. He didn't look back.

"No, no. He hasn't, Tippy. It's fine. He's gone now," Agatha said, bewildered. She reluctantly placed a hand on Tippy's shoulder. She never knew what to do when someone was upset but this seemed like a good start.

Another tap at the window made both girls jump.

Leopold.

Agatha slid the window open for the second time that evening. "I said four knocks."

Leopold didn't smile. "After what I just saw, I wasn't exactly thinking about how many times to knock."

"Did you see him?"

"Who was that?" asked Leopold. "He ran off toward the front of the cemetery."

"That's where he's buried," Tippy whispered.

“Where who’s buried?” asked Leopold again.

“My ghost,” said Agatha. “My newest assignment.”

“Finally!” Leopold said, as if he’d been awaiting an assignment too. “Are you going to give me the...what was that word you used? Deets?”

Agatha crinkled her face. *Never using that word again.* “Well, I—”

Agatha heard her mother’s slippers shuffling down the hallway toward the bathroom just feet from her door. She motioned for Tippy to hide under her bed and whispered to Leopold, “Parade tomorrow. Meet you at your house at six. Give you the deets then.” Gross. She couldn’t even help herself.

“Yeah, but where are we going tomorrow night?” Leopold whispered.

“The haunted hospital on Back Bay,” she said, yanking down the blinds, not waiting for his reaction.

CHAPTER 16
A SURPRISE VISITOR

On Tuesday, a short trip to Tippy's house was necessary as items from the original summoning needed to be collected: the Dark Library candle, the matches and the small wooden box. Tippy threw them in a purple backpack she tightened around her shoulders.

"Want to put the book in my summoning bag too? Just so everything is together?" she asked Agatha.

Summoning bag. Agatha was caught off guard by the casual name Tippy had suddenly given her backpack. "No, it's alright," she said. Agatha had stuffed it in her own backpack. She didn't want to part with the book whatsoever.

They walked to the beach and one street over to Leopold's, parade attendees already gathering and mingling about. Agatha hated the parades and all the debauchery that went with them, but she pretended to be interested this year, promising her mother she would attend the one she was riding in. Luckily her mother's float was the Krewe of Jupiter parade, so Agatha could both attend and disappear, hiding amongst all the Mardi Gras revelers and her mother would not even notice. She also told her mother she would be staying the evening at Tippy Trinkle's house. Anita Anxious had cocked an eyebrow but ultimately seemed happy Agatha had friends and asked no questions.

At exactly six, Tippy and Agatha found themselves waiting in the empty lot across the street from Leopold's house, but he didn't come out. They waited five more minutes before Agatha knocked on his window. Leopold appeared, holding up a finger. He looked busy. Finally, he joined them from behind his house, a black backpack on his shoulders over his black jacket, black pants and black tennis shoes.

"I'm a ninja tonight," he said, referring to his outfit. He retrieved two bikes, orange and blue, from his carport. "One of you will have to ride on the bike with me, I guess," he said, clearly looking at Agatha.

"I'm not sure we should use the bikes," Agatha said. "We might blend in better on foot."

Leopold nodded. "True, but then there's no escape if we get into trouble."

Agatha shrugged. "I run pretty fast."

"I'm faster," he said, before adding, "And there's always trouble."

Agatha smiled. "True."

"Also, why's it always got to be some scary place?"

"Ghost stuff, I guess," Agatha shrugged.

"I mean next time can it like a Build-A-Bear or Taco Sombrero or something?"

Agatha thought for a moment. "You mean an empty restaurant with chairs and tables that move on their own? Or what, a doll store with stuffed animals coming alive at night and skittering around on two legs? No thanks."

"Yeah, nevermind. Maybe a playground?"

Agatha shook her head. "Creaking swings, rusty slides, a merry go round that moves without being touched."

"Ok, I give up," he said. "Everything has a creep factor."

"Yes, it does. Anyway, what were you doing?" she asked as the trio walked to the very end of Leopold's street and crossed over to Forrest Avenue.

"When?"

"In your bedroom just now. You looked busy."

"Oh." He paused and Agatha noted the hesitation. "Just some research from the library. I went yesterday."

"Something for school?"

"No." More hesitation.

"Are you a nerd? You're always at the library," Agatha teased.

"Why yes, yes I am," Leopold smiled. "No doubt. And so? Nerds are cool."

"Oh yeah?"

"Yeah. Because of their superior intelligence, they know everything. And if they don't know, they'll find out. So, THEN they know everything. Which means they pretty much always know everything." Leopold was suddenly serious. "Who wouldn't want to be a nerd?"

Agatha nodded in agreement.

"Anyway, it was something for you," he added.

"What?"

"What I'm working on. It's something for you."

"What is it?"

"Now why would I tell you that? It's not done yet."

"It's not mushy, is it?" She had to ask. Mushy was gross and ruined friendships, or so she figured.

"No way. Not mushy. Intellectual." Leopold said, smiling. "Nerd-ish."

"The parade starts on Caillavet Street," Tippy said, and Agatha shuddered at the name. *Caillavet*. "It will go down Porter, then back up Forrest. So, let's just go down to the end of Forrest. That's where the hospital is, anyway."

The parade had already started when they arrived, and they weaved their way in between loud and raucous attendees. For a few minutes, they stood on the corner of Forrest and Bayview feigning interest in the day's festivities and attempting to blend in.

Agatha glanced at the hospital, her mind wandering back toward her childhood memories of Big. Why did he come to her all those years ago when she couldn't have offered him any help? She tried to remember if he'd told her anything of importance back then, her memories mismatched and mushed together, cloudy like the waters of Back Bay, which coincidentally was right across the street from where she was now standing. Her thoughts were drifting to what would be found at the bottom of the bay if they ever drained it when suddenly a pair of purple beads hit her in the arm.

"Is that your mom?" Leopold shouted over the crowd.

"Yes!" Agatha held her hands up, and her mother threw her a set of heavy beads with a fleur-de-lis at the bottom. She handed them to Leopold and waved to her mother. The evening was going as planned. Her mother had seen her and knew she was where she said she'd be. She wouldn't be later—the rest of the evening was a lie—but that didn't matter. They would try to hurry.

As the crowd dispersed, Agatha, Tippy and Leopold crossed the street and sat on the lone pier across from the hospital, waiting until it was completely dark before entering. Leopold paused from playing with the prize set of beads around his neck. All three stared in awe at the looming structure before them as the setting sun melted into the murky waters of the bay, trading its golden light for a place to sleep among the fish.

Built in the early 1960s on Back Bay, the five-story hospital had been abandoned for a few years, and nature had started to take ownership of it. Trees and limbs littered the top of the overhang that once served as the emergency room drop off, grass crept in between the cracks in the cement of the empty parking lot, and vines wound themselves around several sides of the building, hugging the hospital as if to say, "Mine!"

Hooligans had also done their fair share of damage, too. Agatha could see graffiti everywhere, and the glass front doors of the emergency room area were completely broken, replaced by several pieces of wood, which separated slightly at the bottom. *An entry point,* she thought.

"Ok, tell me," said Leopold. "What are we doing here?"

He threw a rock into the water from the pier, and it landed with a clunk, its ripples wrinkling the dense, brown water with a thickness reminiscent of syrup on pancakes.

Agatha felt like she was repeating herself with the story she'd just told Tippy the night before. "I had an imaginary friend about five years ago named Big."

"Named what?"

"Big. Anyway, he's returned now, and he's my assignment, but I'm not sure what he wants."

"Ok, where's the scary part?" Leopold threw another rock, this one smaller.

"Scary part?"

"Yeah, like the last ghost we helped had no head and we had to make a trip to Deer Island in the middle of the night. What's wrong with this one?"

"Well, I don't know," Agatha said, joining him at the pier's railing. "But Tippy's been seeing him too."

"He had no head?" Tippy interrupted. "You know what? I don't want to know."

"Whoa, really? Do all of us see ghosts or something?" Leopold brushed off his hands.

"I don't know," Agatha continued. "You saw him last night in my backyard, right, Leopold?"

"That was Big?"

Agatha nodded. "And Tippy's been seeing him at her house and other places, but he's different to her. He's mean for some reason. It's weird. He seems like he's asking me for help but he's been threatening Tippy, which is what I need to figure out. I don't think Tippy is a Perceiver. I think she sees Big, I mean Henry, because he's her brother."

"What does that have to do with anything?" Leopold asked.

"Something Aunt Hattie told me. Just because you see ghosts doesn't mean you're a Perceiver. Most of the time it's a family member's ghost, so that's why you see them. I think that's why Tippy is seeing Henry."

"Or maybe it's because I conjured him."

"Did you just say 'conjure?'" asked Leopold, looking at Tippy.

Tippy nodded. "I used that book I stole from Agatha's aunt, remember? I conjured him. And I think he's mad at me because of it."

"So, we're here to sort of 'put him back,' I guess." Agatha wasn't totally sure any of this would work, and it reflected in her voice. "He died at the hospital, and the book said to go to the place where the person died to reverse the summoning."

Agatha checked her watch and looked back toward Forrest Avenue. The street was mostly empty except for a few stragglers hanging around after the parade. They were not the least bit interested in the three teenagers on the pier. "It's dark enough. Time to go."

"So, this is what happens when you try to contact a dead person? Noted." Leopold attempted to lighten the mood with sarcasm.

Agatha turned to face him. "Big, my former imaginary friend, is Tippy's dead brother, Henry. You figured that out, right?"

Leopold shook his head, "Yes. Also, wow. What a coincidence."

The trio hurried across the street, finding their way to the broken doors of the emergency room entrance. They pulled back the soft, decaying wood that served as a door prohibiting entry to the hospital, the rotting wood no match for teenagers on a mission.

Leopold held the wood open for Agatha to enter first as a deep, familiar voice stopped them in their tracks.

"What in the world are you guys doing?

Dorian Doom.

CHAPTER 17
THE OLD HOSPITAL

Every aspect of the evening had been planned and predicted and accounted for except one minor thing: running into someone they knew at the abandoned hospital.

"What are you doing here?" Leopold asked Dorian.

"I was at the parade. Saw you guys while I was walking home. My Uncle lives right here." He pointed to the street behind the hospital.

Of course he does, Agatha thought.

"Ok, so what are you guys doing?" Dorian repeated.

Everyone looked at Agatha to provide the answer. She stared at him, hard, deciding what information to tell him and what to keep secret. On one hand, Dorian had seen Blanche Caillavet, so he was no stranger to ghosts. On the other hand, Agatha wasn't sure whether he was a Perceiver and would understand that she had "missions," and she was already tired of having to repeat the same story.

She bit the side of her lip, deciding to go with the simplest, most genuine answer and crossed her fingers Dorian wouldn't ask too many questions. "We're here to find a ghost." When he didn't answer her, she made it more lighthearted. "Wanna join us?"

"Is it the Woman in White?" he asked, lowering his voice.

"No way."

"Who?" asked Tippy.

Agatha ignored her.

He shrugged. "Ok, I'm in. As long as it's not her. I don't ever want to see her again." He bent down and helped Leopold hold open the rotting wood. As Agatha eased her small body into the opening, she passed through the cloud of tension emanating from Leopold. He didn't like Dorian, but she didn't know why. *Maybe it's a dude thing.* One of her stockings snagged on the wood, tearing a hole near her ankle.

Tippy Trinkle followed closely behind, then Leopold, and finally Dorian, who resituated his baseball cap backwards on his head.

Once inside, they found themselves in a small waiting room with overturned chairs and small end tables. Leopold clicked on his flashlight. Tippy stayed close behind Agatha, her hand sometimes grabbing Agatha's elbow. Agatha smiled. Never did she expect to be leading the charge with a terrified Tippy Trinkle in tow.

Dorian lagged at the end of their line using the light from his cell phone, and Agatha was glad to have the strongest member of their group keeping watch at the rear. "Well now I wish I'd worn tennis shoes," she heard him say. She looked down at her own slip-on black shoes and agreed, though she didn't own any tennis shoes. She eyed the hole in the stocking. Maybe it was time for sneakers *and* pants.

A corridor stretched out in front of them, littered with broken glass, dirt, leaves, and cardboard boxes. Multiple rooms and offices lined either side of the long hallway, and the group read the placards adorning each door as they passed them. Waiting area, admit, insurance, general lab, conference, admin, and more waiting areas, each room a mess of discarded medical equipment, soggy papers, hospital beds, pens and pencils and clothes like the hospital had just stopped operating one day, ousting all their patients and staff in a hurry.

The building was humid and dank, the walls shimmering with moisture. The cold February air coupled with the Mississippi humidity hung in the halls like a melancholy mood of things long forgotten, untouched and abandoned. It was a place of prayers unanswered, sudden goodbyes, abrupt endings, tears and tragedies. And all those feelings and memories still clung to every wall, hid in every corner, could be felt in every stairwell, elevator and crevice of the Back Bay Hospital. *This is what death must feel like,* Agatha thought, *if being dead feels like anything*.

Agatha swallowed. This was a place where some lives had begun, and others had ended. Where babies had taken their first breath and others had taken their last. It was a place where some had gotten well, and others hadn't. And indeed, it was a place where some had come knowing they would never leave. The hospital still smelled of all those people, Agatha thought. Every hospital probably did.

Leopold shone his light to the end of the corridor which presented them with a choice: one hallway on the left and one on the right, both with more rooms where discarded things had likely been left to rot. Immediately to their right was a set of elevators and stairs. "Well, left, right, or up. Those are our choices."

"Do you know where he died?" Agatha asked Tippy.

"He?" said Dorian.

Tippy shook her head. "I have a memory of being in a hospital room, like my own room. With a bed and a nightstand and stuff. But I wouldn't know what room number that was."

"He?" Dorian asked again.

Leopold shined his flashlight directly in Dorian's face. "It's Tippy's twin brother, ok? He died here a long time ago. She tried to call up his ghost. It worked and he's mad and we're here to put him back."

"Ok, ok, I got it," Dorian said, covering his eyes. "I mean, I still have questions—lots of questions—but ok."

Agatha put her hand on his arm, surprised at her own brazenness. Touching a boy? Especially Dorian Doom? "It's complicated," she said. Dorian nodded.

"Let's go up," said Leopold sharply, noticing their interaction.

Agatha shined her flashlight into one of the elevators, its doors already ajar like a dark, hungry mouth begging them to enter.

"No way," said Dorian.

Leopold took a step back. "I'm not getting in there," said Leopold.

"Of course we're not getting in there," said Agatha.

"What is that?" Tippy pointed a shaking finger at an object in the corner.

Agatha timidly looked inside the elevator, where her cone of light rested upon something normally seen in operating hospitals. Something which, generally speaking, had no creep factor to it. But when placed in an abandoned, dark, silent hospital, an antique, wooden wheelchair had the ability to put goosebumps on your arms and a pit in your stomach. *Even normal, everyday items could become scary in the right setting*, Agatha thought. The wheelchair, its wicker seat cracked and torn, oddly faced the corner as though its invisible occupant were being punished.

"I'm taking the stairs," Agatha said, not waiting for anybody to follow behind her. She knew they would if they were smart, and almost everyone in her company this evening seemed to be smart. Well, mostly.

"Yeah, me too," Leopold said, heading to the stairwell.

The doors to the elevator remained open as the foursome ascended the stairs to the second floor where they found patient rooms. Most were empty, but one or two rooms had the odd, abandoned beds with wheels, still silently waiting for a patient that would never come.

Dorian kicked at a pile of leaves in one of the hallways. "Where is all this coming from?"

"I think some of the windows are broken," replied Leopold, as he peeked in two more patient rooms.

"Third floor?" Agatha asked, and they ascended the stairs again, Leopold leading the way, with the girls sandwiched in the center. They were disappointed to find the rest of the floors of the hospital were nothing but patient rooms and nurse's stations. Tippy sat down in one of the hallways on the fifth floor, her head in her hands. "It could be any of these rooms. There's like, a hundred and fifty of them."

Agatha, Leopold and Dorian joined her on the floor, sitting cross legged in a circle. Agatha produced the book from her backpack. "Let's just try it here. Maybe we should do it on each floor. There are five floors, so we'll only have to do it five times. Let's turn off our flashlights," she directed.

Tippy opened her backpack and set the candle and matches and wooden box in a neat little pile. "Who's going to do it?"

"I think you have to, Tippy."

The others watched as Tippy scratched a match against the side of the box and lit the candle. Leopold and Agatha turned off their flashlights, and Agatha pushed the book toward Tippy, who took a deep breath. She held her hand over the open flame and when she could stand it no longer, rested her palm on the book's cover. Agatha, Leopold and Dorian watched in amazement.

"Henry Trinkle," Tippy said, taking another breath. "June eleventh. I return you to slee—"

Tippy didn't finish the final word of her sentence before a giggle down the hallway sent everyone to their feet. Tippy crouched behind Dorian as Leopold clicked on his flashlight. The light revealed nothing at the end of the hallway.

"We definitely heard that, all of us, right?" Leopold said. Everyone nodded their heads except Dorian, whose blue eyes were wild with uncertainty.

"Keep going," Agatha said to Tippy. "Finish."

"Slee...Sleeppp." Tippy's voice was shaking. "I return you to sleep," she said quickly, to get the entire sentence in for good measure.

Another giggle, this time closer.

"Ok what's going on?" Dorian said, his voice high with concern.

Tippy gripped Agatha's sleeve. "Let's go down a floor and finish it there!"

Agatha debated. When the book said the spell needed to be said 'thrice,' did that mean three times in the exact spot where Big died or would three separate spots in the hospital be ok? She didn't know but wasn't waiting for another giggle. "Ok," Agatha said, she and Leopold gathering the items as quickly as they could.

Tippy slid her small hand into Agatha's as they descended the stairwell, Leopold leading as usual and Dorian in the back, facing behind them with his phone's flashlight. She gripped Tippy's warm hand and raced down to the fourth floor, setting up the items again in the long, filthy corridor.

Tippy and Agatha knelt while the boys remained standing. Tippy held her hand over the open flame again, immediately putting it on the book and saying, "Henry Trinkle. June—" Again, she was unable to finish. From the darkness above her, a shadowy figure crawled down the wall and squatted next to Tippy, his hand reaching forward to extinguish the candle.

Tippy screamed.

"What? What happened?" said Dorian, pointing his light at the candle.

Tippy grabbed the sleeve of Agatha's dress again. "I can't do this! I can't!"

"What happened?" Dorian shouted again over Tippy's pleas.

"You didn't see the hand?" Leopold said. His eyes met Agatha's, and she could tell he was afraid.

"A hand?" Dorian exclaimed. "I'm done. I want to leave!"

"Wait a second!" Agatha screamed. She grabbed Tippy's hand from her dress and squeezed it. "Light the candle again."

"I...I can't!"

"Yes, you can. You have to!" She thrust the pack of matches toward Tippy who tried to light a single match with trembling hands. It took four tries. "Keep your light on the candle," she told Dorian.

The candle flickered to life for the third time, and Agatha breathed a small sigh of relief. "Repeat your last sentence," she told Tippy.

"Hen...Henry Trink...Trinkle, June elev....June eleventh. I re...return you to sleep."

The foursome was still while they waited for something to happen. The candle's flame moved with Tippy's rapid breath and then was still. Agatha whispered to Tippy, her eyes on the candle, "Say it again."

"Here?" said Tippy.

Agatha nodded. "Yes, just get it over with. Either it'll work or it won't."

Tippy held her hand over the candle but before she could begin, she heard a whisper.

A low growl from above her. *"STOP."*

"Don't look up!" Agatha said, urging Tippy to continue.

A hiss and another growl. *"STOP IT."*

"Tippy, keep going!" Agatha said, louder.

Tippy's eyes drifted toward the ceiling where she saw brother, attached to the ceiling tiles by his hands and feet.

"Stop it," he whispered angrily, leaping down from the ceiling and snatching the book in his mouth before running down the corridor on all fours like a wild animal.

"No! Big! Stop!" screamed Agatha, immediately on her feet. She threw her backpack at Dorian who looked confused but caught it in one hand. "Get the candle and matches!" She ran after the figure which bounded into a darkened stairwell and jumped, skipping every step until it landed on the floor below.

"I'm right behind you!" Leopold yelled to Agatha. Within seconds he joined her, and they descended the stairs in pursuit of the shadow.

Once they reached the first floor, they found themselves right where they'd begun their journey, in the corridor near the lobby, facing the elevators which housed the decrepit wheelchair. Dorian and Tippy soon joined Agatha and Leopold, Tippy out of breath and Dorian now carrying both backpacks.

"Where'd he go?" Agatha asked Leopold.

Dorian's voice permeated with anger. "Will someone please tell me what is going on?"

Leopold looked at Agatha, a realization spreading over both their faces. "You can't see him, can you?" he said.

"See who?" Dorian said, his bewildered eyes on Agatha.

"So....so you're not a Perceiver?" Agatha said.

"I'm not a what?"

Leopold snapped his fingers and looked at Agatha. "I knew it."

"Everybody, stop for a second," Dorian said, throwing the backpacks at Agatha's feet. "Was there a ghost up there just now?"

Everybody nodded.

"So, we are chasing a ghost I can't see?"

"We don't have time to explain, but Leopold and I can see ghosts. We're Perceivers," Agatha said, picking up her black backpack and handing the purple one to Tippy.

"Well how come Tippy can see it, then?"

Agatha shrugged. "I'm guessing because she did the spell and woke him up. Or because he's her brother." Truly, Agatha didn't understand, nor did she have all the answers. This was not the Big she knew. He had never been angry or mischievous or growled at her. He'd never been... scary. She turned to Tippy. "Is this how he is to you?"

Tippy shook her head. "Yes."

"Well, great." Dorian threw up his hands. "So, I'm the only one who can't see the ghost, then. How come I saw the other one at the mask shop?"

"Um, guys?" Tippy said, pointing. "The wheelchair..."

They peered inside the elevator. This time, the antique wheelchair faced them, a crinkled piece of paper sitting on the wheelchair's seat. They looked at each other, wondering who among them would be brave enough to step inside the elevator and retrieve the note.

Leopold read everyone's minds. "I'll do it." He handed his flashlight to Agatha who shone the light on the piece of paper. Leopold picked it up by a corner and read it. Agatha saw him swallow.

"What? What does it say?" she said, knowing full well she didn't want to know.

"It's just an arrow,'" Leopold said. "Pointing down."

"What does that mean?" said Tippy, her hand now on Agatha's arm.

"Or is it pointing up?" Leopold turned the paper over in his hands.

Dorian held up a finger and stepped into the elevator with Leopold. He looked at the buttons, satisfied. "There's a floor beneath this one, and I bet he wants us to meet him down there."

"But what is down there?" said Tippy.

Dorian motioned for them to follow him down the stairwell. "It's where I imagine all ghosts would be. The morgue."

CHAPTER 18
THE WAILING

"But what is the plan?" Tippy said. "Like, once we get down there?"

"Hold the door," Dorian said. He descended the stairs, disappearing for a moment. When he returned, he motioned for them to follow. "Ok, come on. There's a door down here."

The silence between the four of them was thick, and Agatha imagined each person's heart was on pace with hers. She could barely breathe. The morgue? That was a place of nightmares during the day. How would it be at night? Empty, she hoped, but she guessed it was never empty. Not really.

They opened the door quietly and were met with the same thick, wet, rotting smell of moisture. Another long corridor stretched out before them.

"I don't want to do this," Tippy shivered, staying in the stairwell.

Agatha grabbed her hand. "You have to," said Agatha. "I've got to get that book back. Plus, we haven't finished the spell, and we can't finish the spell without the book."

"Why can't she stay and wait for us?" said Dorian.

"Because she has to be the one to say the words for the third time," Leopold said, giving him a look. "Agatha already said that."

Again, they assumed the same lineup with Leopold in the front, the girls in the center, and Dorian in the back. Leopold shone his flashlight down a small alcove right near the elevator where an overturned desk chair was spending eternity.

They tiptoed down several corridors, past closed doors they assumed would be of no interest to Big. Storage, Housekeeping, Staff Dining, Linen and Sewing, Laundry, Mechanical. Tippy kept her eyes toward the floor, nearly shut, her hand again in Agatha's. At last, they found themselves looking down one final hallway with two remaining rooms, both of which presented the dilemma of which to enter: Morgue and Autopsy.

"Which one?" Leopold said.

"Morgue," said Dorian.

"Autopsy," Agatha said, to avoid the morgue.

"Neither," said Tippy.

Leopold's flashlight flickered and dimmed, and he smacked it with the palm of his hand. "Let's open both doors and look inside. Back up just a little."

He gently turned the silver knob to the Autopsy room and gave the door a push. No one stepped inside, but all four of them could tell the room was empty. Unlike the rest of the hospital, nothing remained in the autopsy room. It was completely cleared of everything. *Minus one or two invisible souls aimlessly wandering the room,* Agatha thought, unhappy they'd been cut into after death. She was absolutely certain they were there.

"It's empty," Dorian said. "I mean, to me it is." He furrowed his darkened brow, and Agatha could tell he was disappointed. "Is it empty to you guys?"

She turned to the door behind her, knowing that's where Big would be anyway. Bad Big? The shadow? What was he and what should she call him? She could see why Tippy had been so desperate to undo the summoning. Agatha wouldn't want this thing visiting her either, and she could only imagine what Tippy had been through the last week.

"Who's going to open the door?" she asked the others. Tippy still had her eyes mostly closed.

"I will," Dorian said, desperate to be useful. He stepped forward and turned the knob, kicking the door open with his foot. "Hello?" he called from the doorway. "We know you're in here."

Unlike the Autopsy room, the morgue wasn't empty. Several flat metal tables with wheels lined the wall to the left. Opposite the tables was one long counter with several sinks. And directly in front of them, at the back of the room, was the item most associated with a morgue: mortuary cabinets that covered the entire wall.

"Are those...?" said Tippy, her eyes now open.

Leopold nodded. "Yeah, the refrigerators where they put dead bodies."

Tippy swallowed, an audible gulp that gurgled down her esophagus and settled in her belly.

Agatha shined her flashlight to the ceiling, where she'd seen Big on the fourth floor. She guessed he could attach himself to anything, which meant he could be anywhere. Her light swept the room left and right. Nothing seemed amiss except for the top right mortuary cabinet, which was the only one slightly ajar, as if having recently been opened.

"Dorian," Agatha directed. "Go open that cabinet."

"Why me?"

"Because you can't see him anyway, so there's nothing to be afraid of."

"Yeah, but what if it attacks me?"

"It won't," Agatha lied. She had no idea what Big would do.

Just then, the sound of pages tearing caught her attention. "Where is that?" Agatha said, her flashlight frantically scanning the room. "Open the cabinet, Dorian!"

Dorian took a deep breath, filling himself with courage, and ran toward the open mortuary cabinet. He yanked the door fully open and backed away. "Got you!" he said but was met with silence. He looked at his comrades. "I, uh, didn't know if something was in there or not."

Agatha continued to scan the room with her flashlight, the beam finally settling on the far corner, where Big was now squatting, his back to her. His shoulders were moving slightly, and she could make out the sounds of crinkling paper. "He's tearing up the book," she whispered to Leopold, both tiptoeing toward Big.

Suddenly, Big froze, turning his head methodically all the way around until his body faced away from Agatha, but his head faced her. She gasped.

"Hello Agatha," he growled, his body finally turning slowly to face the same direction as his head. He crawled on all fours, dragging the book in one hand. "Have you been waiting for me?"

"Tippy, say...say the words..." she stammered, beginning to retreat. She kept her flashlight on Big. Tippy said nothing, her eyes on her brother.

"How long can you wait, Agatha?"

"Tippy!" she said, more urgent this time.

Big snarled, several droplets of saliva running down his chin. "I have all of eternity."

"What?" Agatha froze.

Big righted himself to two feet, a menacing smile still planted on his lips, his eyes wild with hunger. He raised his hand and threw the book at Agatha with a swiftness she didn't expect. It hit her in the chest, and she stumbled backwards, but Leopold was in front of her before she knew it. He threw the book to Dorian who again caught it with one hand, and he shoved Agatha and Tippy out the door. They all scrambled for the stairwell, their screams piercing the empty hallways and echoing back to them like boomerangs.

When they reached the first floor, Dorian slammed the stairwell door, but they could hear Big's unmistakable footsteps bounding behind them. They ran for the hospital's front entrance, everyone screaming, Dorian clutching the book tightly in his hands, the boys pushing the girls toward the rotting wood which separated them from the outside world and what they perceived would be safety. Agatha dove for the opening with Tippy tripping over her outside. Leopold and Dorian tore the wood from the door as they exited, their arms bloody with scratches and splinters, the four of them breathless as they scrambled on hands and knees across the street.

When they reached the end of the pier, they watched in horror as Big, now walking on two feet, calmly crossed the road in their direction, a wicked smile smeared across his angry face. He didn't pause to look both ways, and Agatha surmised drivers wouldn't see him anyway. His calm, methodical approach felt apocalyptic, as if nothing, earthly or beyond, could stop him.

As he advanced, he dropped to all fours and giggled.

"Big! Stop it!" Agatha screamed. "Why are you being like this? Tippy! Say the words! Now!"

"But I don't have the candle—"

"NOW!"

"I return you to sleep!"

"Again!" Agatha urged her as Big crawled forward on all fours, his fingernails scratching the wood of the pier.

"I return you to sleep! I return you to sleep!" Tippy screamed, her hands over her ears and her eyes tightly shut.

Big continued, unaffected by Tippy's words, and began to laugh, hoarsely, as the foursome were at the end of the pier with nowhere else to go. Suddenly, Leopold stepped in front of Agatha and Tippy, shining his flashlight in Big's face. He looked at Agatha, "Maybe a Perceiver needs to say it, Agatha."

"Henry Trinkle," Leopold began. "June eleventh. I return you to sleep!" He kept his flashlight on Big, whose eyebrows were arched and feral, his orange curls aggressively bouncing against his head which twitched in small spasms as he inched his way forward. And he continued to laugh, a dry, crusty cough of a cackle which Agatha felt she'd heard somewhere before.

Leopold looked over his shoulder at Agatha, his eyes wild with distress. "I'm going to throw him in the water."

"No!" Agatha yelled, but she was too late.

"Run!" Leopold yelled, but nobody did. Agatha and Tippy froze, their arms around each other. Dorian gripped the side of the pier, uncertain what was happening.

Leopold lunged toward Big who suddenly stopped and smiled, an awareness in his eyes that wasn't there before. He stood on two feet and welcomed Leopold's approach as Leopold pushed Big over the side of the pier. Leopold let out a scream as his hands touched Big's body, falling to his knees and exhaling air as if the wind were knocked out of him. Big landed in the water with a splash, the murky liquid accepting him into its depths.

Agatha ran to the side of the pier as Big's face sunk below the surface of the water, changing momentarily to the most wicked of faces. Grey skin, wrinkles, yellow eyes. Tendrils of white hair briefly appeared, wriggling and writhing in the water like worms dying in the sun. Black teeth smiled back at Agatha from behind grey lips before sinking into the darkness.

Blanche Caillavet.

Agatha gasped and backed away. "Leopold?" He was still kneeling in the same position as when he'd first touched Big. His back was to her, and Agatha approached him, apprehensively. His body offered no signs of movement, and Agatha wondered if he was breathing.

"What's wrong with him?" Dorian broke the silence.

Agatha crouched beside Leopold, now seeing his eyes were completely white and pupilless, his mouth open. His jaw slack. She touched his arm, and it was cool. Her hands grasped Leopold's shoulders, and she shook him, but she got no response. Back Bay was silent, except for the water nudging itself against the pier and a few stray cars on the roads in the distance. And a piercing cry from a thirteen-year-old girl named Agatha Anxious.

"*Leopollllllldddd*!" she wailed.

CHAPTER 19
THE THIRD EYE

Agatha wasn't sure how she managed to dial Tobie's number with trembling fingers, but she did.

"Hello?" he picked up on the first ring as if he had nothing better to do.

"I need you to come pick us up."

"From where?"

"The old hosp—" she caught herself. Tobie probably wouldn't know where that was. "I'll give you the address."

"And who is 'us'?"

Agatha didn't answer. Instead, she hung up, betting on the fact Tobie would come regardless. Wouldn't he?

"What happened?" Leopold asked after a few moments, clearly dazed. His green irises and their black pupils had returned, but he was fatigued, and his expression was one of complete confusion.

"I don't know," Agatha answered honestly. Her hand was on his arm again, and thankfully, it was warm this time. She helped him to his feet where he was surprisingly steady. "You threw Big into the water," she said, omitting the part where Big's face had turned into Blanche's.

Leopold nodded his head. "Yes. I remember that."

They walked to the corner of Forrest Avenue and waited for Tobie. Dorian and Tippy were completely silent, processing the night's events in different ways. Tippy with fear and apprehension of her brother, wondering if they'd been successful. Dorian in complete confusion, wondering what in the world had happened.

"I'm just going to walk to my uncle's," Dorian said, as Tobie pulled up, the truck sputtering to a stop and nearly dying. He handed the girls their backpacks and headed toward the street behind the hospital in a daze. "That book is in your bag, Agatha," he called, not looking back.

Agatha helped Leopold into the front seat while she and Tippy took a seat in the bed of the truck. The abruptness of the evening's ending left Agatha feeling vacant, an unfinished business hanging between them. Many questions and no answers.

"Well?" Tobie finally broke the silence between them after they'd dropped off Tippy and Leopold. "I'm guessing you told your parents you were doing something other than what you were really doing. And by the way, what exactly *were* you doing?"

Agatha turned to him, his eyes genuinely curious, not reprimanding. "Dealing with things you don't believe in."

Many things with Tobie required no explanation, kind of like Aunt Hattie. Often, Agatha could speak in code or say as little as possible, and he seemed to understand, this time included. Tobie nodded. "Ah.

More ghosts, eh?" He shifted the truck into another gear as they turned onto Azalea Street and parked in Agatha's driveway.

She nodded.

"And did you find what you were looking for?"

She nodded again. "Kind of."

Tobie smirked.

"Forget it," Agatha said, popping open the passenger door.

"Ok, ok, ok," Tobie held a hand up. "Seriously, what did you find?"

"Are you going to make fun of me?" Agatha was dying to talk to someone else about this other than Leopold. Aunt Hattie would've been her first choice, but of course that was not a possibility. "I guess growing up with Aunt Letty makes you that way, huh?"

Tobie turned off the truck's ignition. "Just like growing up around Aunt Hattie made you *that* way?" He leaned back on the headrest and stared out the windshield, thoughtful. "Aunt Hattie was fun, from what I remember. Sometimes she'd try to play little pretend games with me when I was growing up, calling me some Southern name...Red? Rhett? Mr. Rhett, I think. And she was Miz Honeysuckle. Not 'Miss,' but 'Miz.' She corrected me on that one time."

Agatha suddenly felt sick, her stomach churning with memories she yearned to forget and ached to hold on to.

"But..." he shrugged. "That's all it is, you know? Pretend. Spells, ghosts, spirits, superstitions. None of it's based in fact, really, and I like facts."

"You...you knew Aunt Hattie?" she managed to utter, her eyes closed to stop the rippling waves of nausea.

Tobie didn't notice. "Of course, I did. She came to visit probably once a year, and she and mom talked all the time over the phone. Like, daily."

Agatha let his words settle in the mushy parts of her brain. Aunt Hattie had visited Aunt Letty? When? The notion Aunt Hattie had a life outside of Agatha and her own shop was news to her. "What games did she play with you?" Agatha purposely omitted the word pretend, certain those games Tobie was describing were *not* pretend.

Tobie shrugged. "Some 'third eye' game. Something like we're all born with this extra eye that allows us to see this other dimension. Like, ghosts and stuff. Most of us haven't used that third eye and don't know how to. I guess I fall into that latter category, and she was trying to teach me how to use it." He yanked the keys from the truck's ignition and opened his door. "But I didn't really care to."

Agatha slid off the seat and made her way into the house, a thumb's cuticle in her mouth. She expertly snipped the dead skin with her front teeth. She threw her backpack on her bed and grabbed a pair of pajamas from her nightstand, opting to take a bath instead of eating. She wasn't really that hungry. Her head lobbed and pounded and felt contorted like those skulls she'd seen in Picasso paintings, burdened by the night's events. She sat on the edge of the tub, watching it fill to the brim with steamy water and a capful of bubbles. When the tub was full, she turned off the water and pulled the shower curtain close to trap the rising steam.

Back in her bedroom, she grabbed Aunt Letty's book from her backpack. She ran her fingers across its intricate, leather cover. What was so special about this book to Aunt Letty? Didn't Tobie just insinuate Aunt Letty wasn't interested in any of this? Then why would she desperately want the book back? Her thoughts drifted to Leopold, and she felt around in her backpack for her phone.

Are you ok? She typed with just her middle finger, noticing the cuticle was snagged at the corner, but refrained from nibbling on it. She waited a few moments for Leopold to respond.

No, I died.

Agatha smiled. *Seriously.*

I'm ok. Thanks for the concern, Agatha Anxious.

Do you feel weird?

Nah. I guess I'm tired.

Maybe nothing happened. Agatha could hope.

Yeah, probably not.

There was a pause where neither knew what else there was to say. *Well, goodnight,* Leopold quickly texted. Agatha flipped her phone closed. He always knew how to end things before they got awkward, a skill not many people had learned in her opinion, and she appreciated it.

She pushed open the bathroom door, shivering as a wave of cool air met her skin. Agatha debated whether to wash her hair and counted how many days it had been since the last time it was washed. Her fingers found their way to a sore spot on her chin. *Great, another pimple,* she said, wiping the steam from the mirror and leaning in close to her reflection. Two small bumps situated themselves right beneath her bottom lip, angry and irritated. Agatha shrugged. *Two isn't bad. At least I don't have pizza face like Dad did.*

She pushed on one of the bumps a few times, finally deciding to leave it alone when a movement caught her eye in the mirror. Behind her, in the tub. Through the clear curtain she could see a figure, its silhouette with orange hair on top appeared to be sitting in the water. The head slowly turned toward her, and Agatha crouched between the sink and the toilet. She stayed perfectly still as the figure held up one finger and started to write in the steam on the curtain, each of the three letters in all caps like usual.

JAR

Agatha remained perfectly still until the figure disappeared into the tub's water, like a melting piece of ice, and even then, she waited a few more moments before peeling back the shower curtain to reveal her bathwater. Nothing. She headed back to her room, her teeth now tearing at the corner of her thumb until she tasted blood in her mouth which she wiped on her clothes.

She grabbed the skull jar off her shelf, careful to avoid using the bloody finger, and gently pulled the two pieces of paper out. She unfurled both and reread their messages.

REMEMBER ME?

and

THERE ARE TWO OF ME.

THERE SHOULDN'T BE.

The second piece of paper dropped from her hands as a light bulb flickered to life in her brain like the July 4th fireworks on Biloxi Beach. Big had told her there were two of him, and she hadn't even listened. This was no puzzle of titanic proportions, nothing to figure out. This was no final exam for a passing score on a report card. This hardly was even a test. Big had simply laid it out to Agatha from the beginning. But why? Why were there two of him? It must have something to do with Tippy.

Agatha put on her pajamas and grabbed Aunt Letty's book, flipping through the chapters again. *Items Needed for Summoning*. No. *The Act of Summoning*. No. She kept flipping until her fingers caught on the epilogue, *A Note on Deceivers*. That word seemed familiar to her when she'd read it with Tippy. It had something to do with Aunt Hattie, she knew. She closed her eyes, squeezing them tightly, and lay back on her bed, the book on her chest, her arms crossed over it. She thought hard for a few minutes. Nothing.

"HattieCat?" she called aloud, surprised the kitty wasn't in her bedroom, but she heard its paws pitter pattering down the hallway at her beckoning. It appeared in her doorway with an inquiring expression.

"Yes?" it seemed to say. It was the first human-like acknowledgement Agatha had received from the cat. She held up the book.

"Deceivers," she said, tapping the cover of the book. "You told me, and I can't remember." A moment passed between Agatha and the cat, neither taking their eyes off the other. "Help me, Aunt Hattie," she whispered.

The cat's white whiskers moved into a smirk, and it jumped onto the bed, nestling its head into the crook of Agatha's neck. She laid her hand on its fur and closed her eyes again, burying her face in its fur. A memory played in her ears like a faraway movie viewed through a kaleidoscope of echoes and colors and feelings.

Noodles. The coziness of Aunt Hattie's small kitchen. And Aunt Hattie herself.

"There will be forces against you. Forces that don't want you to succeed. Forces that don't want the dead to get their help."

Aunt Hattie's silky voice brought tears to Agatha's closed eyes, pooling in the corner near her nose, and she made no effort to wipe them away.

"What kind of forces?" Agatha heard herself say.

"You never know," Aunt Hattie answered. *"Mostly, it takes the shape of a person. Someone or something doing the evil work of the evil dead. Deceivers, they're called."*

Agatha gasped, her hands flying to her chest and her eyes open and wild. HattieCat leapt from the bed and disappeared down the hallway.

It all was coming together in front of Agatha's eyes, nuggets of information, piece by piece forming a complete picture. Big appearing differently to Tippy. The evil face when Big sank into the dark water of Back Bay. Was the Big that Tippy was seeing a Deceiver, somehow controlled or manipulated by Blanche Caillavet? Maybe that version of Big *was* Blanche Caillavet. And the real Big needed Agatha's help to get rid of the Deceiver.

Agatha furiously flipped to the epilogue of Aunt Letty's book, stopping on the page which read *A Note on Deceivers*, she nodded to herself. She was finally getting somewhere. A light had flickered on, illuminating her path, an avenue toward helping Big and perhaps another piece of mirror glass. She sucked in a triumphant breath and turned the page, her shaking fingers coming to rest on the torn edges of paper near the spine of the book. She had to touch their shredded pieces several times to believe it.

The epilogue had been ripped out.

CHAPTER 20
GAME NIGHT

Wednesday, although a holiday from school, was chore day for Agatha, and late that afternoon, she begrudgingly set about wiping the baseboards with a bowl of Lysol water and a ragged washcloth. It was her least favorite chore, one which her parents insisted she do every few months, and especially today since her mother had announced the evening would be spent as family game night with her coworker Penny and her son. She'd saved the baseboards for the last chore of the day.

"Scrabble?" her mother presented the board game's empty box to her as Agatha finished the second corner of the dining room.

"No way," Agatha said, wringing out the dirty washcloth of dust and Macbeth's black hair. After the Deer Island Ghost, she wasn't sure she could ever play Scrabble again.

Anita Anxious sighed. It was the fourth game she'd presented to Agatha. "Well, that leaves Taboo."

"Ok," Agatha nodded. "Do we have an even number of people?"

"Yep. Your dad, me, Tobie, you, Penny, and her son. Maybe you and her son can be on a team." She winked, tucking a long strand of dirty blonde hair behind her ear.

Agatha rolled her eyes. "No."

"Oh, lighten up, Agatha. It'll be fun." She peered at Agatha through her large brown glasses, which sat at the end of her nose.

"What's Penny's last name?" said Agatha, trying to determine whether she already knew Ms. Penny's son.

Her mother cocked her head to one side, thinking. "You know, I can't remember. Something weird."

Agatha wrung out the washcloth again. "I'm done. And I have homework to do, anyway." She dumped the brown water into the garbage can and placed the bowl in the sink. "Oh, Mom?"

"Yes, honey?"

"Do you think you could pick me up some...some jeans or something next time you go shopping?"

A little smile formed in her mother's eyes. Agatha could tell she didn't want to give too much away, though her words did. "Absolutely."

"Thanks."

"Oh, and try to be done with your homework soon. They'll be here in about thirty minutes."

Agatha didn't respond, planting herself at her desk. She opened her binder to a fresh sheet of paper and flipped to the photos folder on her phone where she'd taken pictures of each of the Black History Month's icons' quotes. She paused to text Leopold.

How are you feeling?

Immediate response. *I told you, I died.*

LOL. Agatha cringed as she typed the acronym knowing full well she wasn't laughing out loud. She waited a minute, finding something to say. *Mom's making me clean the house. Apparently, we're having a family game night with her coworker Penny and her weird son. Save me.*

Agatha watched as three bubbles appeared, indicating Leopold was typing a response, but no response came. After a few moments, he stopped typing. Then:

I like games. Why is the lady's son weird?

Agatha thought for a moment. *I don't know. I just felt like saying that because I'm a mean person.*

You're not mean, Agatha Anxious. Just weird. But weird is good.

She smiled and flipped back to the photographs folder, considering each picture and quote one by one.

> *Darkness cannot drive out darkness; only light can do that. Hate cannot drive out hate; only love can do that.*
>
> *– Martin Luther King, Jr.*

> *I would unite with anybody to do right and with nobody to do wrong.*
>
> *– Frederick Douglas*

> *I feel safe in the midst of my enemies, for the truth is all powerful and will prevail.*
>
> *– Sojourner Truth*

Every great dream begins with a dreamer. Always remember you have within you the strength, the patience, and the passion to reach for the stars to change the world.

-Harriet Tubman

It's when we forget ourselves that we accomplish tasks that are most likely to be remembered.

-Bessie Coleman

You must never be fearful about what you are doing when it is right.

-Rosa Parks

No individual has any right to come into the world and go out of it without leaving behind him distinct and legitimate reasons for having passed through it.

-George Washington Carver

Agatha put her phone on her desk and rested her head in her hands, thinking of some small act that would represent any of these quotes, the bare minimum that she could get away with. After all, it was due on Monday. Had she done anything over the break that would count for something? Well, she *had* done something over the break, but nothing she could write about for a class assignment without sounding like a complete fool. She sighed. A lie would have to do.

She grabbed a piece of college lined notebook paper and a pencil and began to write.

I am choosing Bessie Coleman's quote "It's when we forget ourselves that we accomplish tasks that are most likely to be remembered" for this report. Over the Mardi Gras break, I decided to volunteer at the local homeless shelter and served some meals.

Agatha immediately crumpled the piece of paper and flicked it into the trashcan. That lie was too much and made her feel like a terrible person. She needed some air and tiptoed down the hallway to Tobie's bedroom, where she rapped her knuckles a few times on the door.

"Come in," he said, turning down his classical music. Tobie was sprawled out on his little bed in a grey sweatsuit, a small black pair of glasses on his face.

"What are you doing?" she asked, looking around his room. The family's tiny third 'junk room' had been greatly improved with its new facelift as Tobie's bedroom. One twin bed on her left, a chipped little thrift store lamp adorning the nightstand next to it. One small bookshelf jammed with books and trinkets. A desk for homework, also from the thrift store, its top scratched and covered with stickers from its former owner. And a few movie posters lined the walls, including one she absolutely hated. Some 1980s movie about a lost extraterrestrial trying to get home to its planet. A weird, large-eyed brown alien stared at her from the wall, its glowing finger pointing her direction.

"I really hate that thing."

"I know. Oh, and I'm waiting on game night."

"What?"

"You asked me what I was doing. I'm waiting for game night. I love board games." Tobie thumbed through a thick paperback titled *The Fountainhead.* He dogeared a page and took off his glasses. "Well, I like strategy games best, like chess. That's my favorite. But I'll play whatever Aunt Anita wants me to."

Agatha smirked. Aunt Anita sounded so weird. She'd spent so much time viewing other people, like Aunt Hattie, as "aunts," that she hadn't considered her own mother to be one to someone else. In Agatha's world, only she had aunts, no one else. And a magical aunt, at that.

Three quick knocks on the front door followed by Macbeth's barking got Agatha's attention and she frowned. "I hate meeting new people."

He shrugged. "Yeah, I'm not much for it either. I don't find many humans worth interacting with because everything is so surface. Not a lot of people have depth, like you Agatha. Well, I mean, I guess you're deep because you're out looking for ghosts at all hours of the night." Tobie playfully rolled his eyes.

"Agatha! Tobie! They're here," her mother called from the living room, and Agatha frowned again.

She heard her father's voice intermingled with a woman's from the hallway, the woman's high and nervous and giggly. She was a fast talker. "Oh yes! Yes. Nice to meet you, Sonny. I'm Penny. Anita and I have been working together for about six months, and let me tell you, she is just the greatest trainer. Work has been so easy. Just delightful, really. Best job I've had in a long time, and that's because of your wife!" Penny continued, and Agatha wondered when she had time for a breath. "Things haven't been easy for us since my dad died a few years ago, but we're making it and honestly, Anita has really made life a lot easier. My son stays a lot by himself while I work, but he's doing well too, aren't you hon?"

The son must've nodded because Agatha heard no response. She held her breath as she rounded the corner into the living room just as Penny was continuing to talk.

"Either way, I had no idea we were so close! We're just a street over on Gill Avenue..."

Agatha's feet led her to the living room quicker than her brain could process what Penny was saying. As she entered, her mother smiled and pointed toward the woman whose brown tightly curled hair bounced lightly against her bony shoulders. The woman smiled big, displaying a neat, tidy collection of brilliantly white teeth. Her son stepped from behind his mother and waved like a three-year-old, a sarcastic grin spread across his tucked in lips.

"Honey, this is Penny. Penny Panic, and her son, Leopold."

CHAPTER 21
TWINS

Agatha cocked her head to the side and looked at her mother. "Mom, Leopold and I have like five classes together."

Both women gasped. "Really? Oh, that's wonderful!"

"Yes, that is wonderful," Penny Panic parroted Anita Anxious. "I'm so glad you have a friend, Leo."

Leo. Agatha didn't like it. That nickname did not fit Leopold at all, but then again, she herself was accustomed to the ridiculous nicknames parents often gave their children and then sometimes called them in public. At least Leopold's nickname was a real name. Sometimes her father called her Boynky and Freedorper, which made Agatha want to jump off a cliff when he accidentally said it in public. *I get Freerdorper, and he gets Leo. Yeah, that's fair.*

"Well, there's no need for more introduction then," her mother laughed. "Please, come in. I made spaghetti and it's ready." She laughed again. "Oh my! I rhymed and I didn't mean to. The spaghetti is ready!" Agatha shook her head. Leopold gave her a "what's with your mom" look, and she shrugged. Nerves.

They hung back while everyone fixed their plates, idle friendly chatter filling the small kitchen. Agatha stepped close to Leopold's ear. "We have work to do."

"I know."

"You do?"

"Well, I'm guessing we didn't do anything successful last night, so there has to be more to do, right?" He was speaking out of the side of his mouth like a ventriloquist.

"We'll talk in my room after dinner."

He nodded and filled a bowl with spaghetti, taking a seat at the small dining room table. Agatha's mother had opened a few folding chairs she kept in the carport to accommodate their guests. Porkchop Cupcake, the lopsided, groaning air conditioner was off, thank Goodness, since it was February, but he still sat guard over the table like a fat, awkward pig, out of place and uncomfortable in his window frame.

"Does everybody know how to play Taboo?" her mother asked.

Sonny Anxious spoke up. "Mind if I sit this one out? I just want to enjoy the spaghetti and watch some tv, if nobody minds?" He looked at the faces around the table, hoping for their blessing.

"Me too," Tobie kindly volunteered. "I mean, if that is ok with you, Aunt Anita? I think you need an even number of people for Taboo, don't you?"

Anita Anxious hesitated. "Oh. Yes, we do. That's fine. Penny and me against Leopold and Agatha, then. Will that work?"

The three of them nodded their heads while Sonny and Tobie took seats on the couch, the television suddenly alive and reporting the evening's news stories.

"Ok, so you draw a card and then describe the word on the card to your partner without saying the word itself and without saying the other five words on the card, too. Really, you're just trying to get your partner to say the word. Does that make sense?"

More nodding of heads. Leopold slurped a long noodle into his mouth.

"Leo," his mother nudged him. "Have some manners." She whispered loud enough for everyone to hear, and Leopold's face turned red. He wiped his mouth with a paper towel.

The next hour was fun, Agatha thought, and she helped herself to two large bowls of spaghetti not spilling even one drop on her dress. Her belly was pleasantly full and made a few happy gurgling noises as she and Leopold tied their mothers in Taboo. When a tiebreaker card was drawn, they watched intently as Penny tried to get Anita to say the word for the win. Agatha turned the timer on for thirty seconds, and Penny flipped the card.

"Oh gosh, um, ok. When you...expire...?"

Anita grimaced. "Die?"

"Um, yes! Ok. Um, this happens."

Anita bit her lip. "Cremation? Burial?"

Penny sighed. "No." She thought for a second. "Ok how about this. You become this. Or well, *can*. You can become this."

Anita put her hand to her chin, deep in thought.

Penny wiped a few of her curls away from her face. "Ok, forget that. You know the old hospital on Back Bay?"

Agatha and Leopold sat up.

"Yeah?"

"It has one of these. Well, I'm sure it has a lot of these."

"A morgue?" Anita looked puzzled.

Penny nodded. "No, more...monstrous things."

Anita shook her head a couple times, feeling the pressure of the ticking timer. "Dead people?"

Leopold's green eyes burned into Agatha's.

Penny's voice got higher again, excited. "Yes! And they are...?" she pointed to the card.

Anita Anxious bit her lip again.

Penny nodded, urging her to keep talking. "They're...." She paused, for effect. "...still there. You know, the little boy."

"A ghost!"

Penny stood up, feeling the impending win. "Yes! And it does what? The thing you just mentioned. It does what?"

Anita stood up too. "Haunt?"

Penny shook her head, her curls falling back in her face. "Yes! Yes! Past tense!"

"Haunted!"

She and Penny did a high five, and Penny bumped Leopold with her shoulder. She smiled at Agatha. "Sorry, kids. Next time."

Agatha's mouth was open, and she looked over at Leopold to find his was too. She couldn't pass up this opportunity. "I'm sorry. Wait. The word on the card is 'haunted'?"

"Yes," Penny took a sip of her room temperature water on the table.

"And what did you just say about the boy?" Leopold interrupted

Agatha, getting the point before she could.

"Oh, some old Biloxi ghost story about a kid ghost being at the old Back Bay hospital. Used to play with elevator buttons and change the thermostat and switch the lights on and off. Playful ghost, I guess." Penny took another sip from her glass. "I had a friend who worked there a few years ago," she added, giving legitimacy to her claim. "Yeah, she used to hear like, phantom giggling and stuff. I think she said he was a twin, and the other kid is still alive. A pair of twins went in, and only one came out. Something like that."

A tingle started in Agatha's throat, and she felt the smallest hint of a recollection, an old little memory buried deep within the folds of her brain attempting to find the surface. Visiting her grandmother at the hospital? Wait, didn't she die there? No, that was too long ago. Visiting someone at the hospital. A sick person. And Big was there too. She could see them pressing all the buttons inside the elevator together.

Agatha excused herself from the table, mentioning her homework again and asking for permission for Leopold to accompany her to her room. "We have the same homework," she told her mother. "So, we're just going to work on it together." She forced a smile.

"Ok, sure. Just keep your door open," Anita Anxious winked at her daughter as Penny joined her in the kitchen to assist with dishes. Agatha rolled her eyes. What were she and Leopold going to do in her room with the door closed? What was the insinuation?

She glared at her mother when Leopold's back was turned and mouthed the words. *Eww*.

Sonny and Tobie were now engrossed in some pirate movie as she and Leopold passed by on their way to Agatha's room. Once in her room, Agatha pulled up the pictures with the quotes again.

"Which one are you doing?" She thumbed through them one by one, still deciding.

"I don't know. I like to do things last minute."

Agatha smiled. "Me too. Procrastination is key."

"For sure. It's when I do my best work," Leopold agreed.

Agatha turned off her phone and arched her head to listen for anything different out in the living room. Several laughs from Anita and Penny told her they were still in the kitchen finishing the dishes. The television's foreboding music indicated the movie's climax, and she knew her father and Tobie were still invested. She grabbed Aunt Letty's book and the skull jar and looked at Leopold.

"I figured something out."

"Okay." He folded his arms, waiting for her to continue.

She pulled the two notes from the jar and showed them to Leopold. "There are two Bigs. One that is the normal one, you know, my childhood imaginary friend, and one—the threatening one—that is appearing to Tippy. The one you threw in the water."

He nodded. "That makes total sense."

"Yeah, and he told me right from the beginning. I feel kind of stupid for not paying attention. And the bad one—er, Bad Big, I guess—is a Deceiver. I think."

"A what?"

"A Deceiver. It was something Aunt Hattie told me about. Essentially, a Deceiver is someone or something working against a Perceiver. But in this case, I think it might be a copy of someone? Just a guess." She hesitated, framing her words as a question, unsure about the truth of any of it. "When you pushed Big into the water, I watched him sink, and when he did, his face turned into...Blanche Caillavet's." She shuddered at the name.

Leopold's bottom lip parted from his top one in surprise. "Really?"

"Yes, I think the Deceiver is being controlled by Blanche." She jammed the corner of her pinky in her mouth and tore away a dry piece of skin.

"And the Deceiver is only here because of Tippy, isn't it?"

Agatha tossed the skin around on her tongue before biting down on it with her front teeth. "Yes. I think so. I can't think of any other reason."

"And Big—the real Big—wants you to get rid of the Deceiver, doesn't he?"

Agatha smiled. "I knew I kept you around for a reason."

Leopold took a seat at her desk. "And how do we do that? Or you, I mean. I guess it has to be you, really. How do you do that?"

Agatha plopped down on her bed, throwing her head back onto the pillow. "That is what I need to figure out." She showed him Aunt Letty's book. "When I first went through the book with Tippy, there was an epilogue about Deceivers. I didn't read it because I'm a dummy. Then we went to the hospital, and when I got home, I opened to the book to find this." She threw the book to Leopold.

He flipped to the end of the book, finding the ragged pages. He looked at Agatha, and slammed the book shut. "Dorian tore that out."

"What?" she said, sitting up.

"Well, he had it, didn't he? For a short time, anyway, when I threw him the book while we were in the morgue. He was carrying both backpacks, too."

Agatha sighed. Leopold didn't like Dorian for some unknown reason, but he had a point. One she hadn't considered. "But I heard the Deceiver tearing pages from the book. When he was in the corner of the morgue."

Leopold thought for a moment. "Fair enough. But I still think Dorian did it."

"But why?"

He shrugged. "I dunno. Just that gut feeling. Never underestimate your gut."

Aunt Hattie had told her something similar months ago, but Leopold's opinion of Dorian was already tainted. How could he make an unbiased assessment?

"Anyway," he said, changing the subject, "back to the real question. "How do we—YOU—get rid of the Deceiver?"

"I don't know." Agatha hesitated for a moment. "Lucius Nikolai appeared to me in a dream recently," she whispered.

"He what?"

"He came to me in a dream, and he told me to 'find the light' or something like that."

"What's that mean?"

"I have no idea. What DOES it mean? I think he's giving me a hint. The light, whatever it is, will get rid of the Deceiver. I just have to find it."

"What could it be?"

Agatha shrugged. "Could be anything. Maybe something in this room, even. I've been thinking about this for days. How can I find the thing I'm looking for if I don't know WHAT it is?"

"Yeah."

"But..." she paused to tear at some hard skin around the callouses on her palm. "...I do know who could answer that."

Leopold's mouth fell open as the realization of her words hit him, and he emphatically shook his head. "No, no, no. Dude, no."

"Yes, yes, yes. Dude, yes."

She curled the small pieces of paper and gently put them back in the skull jar, which she neatly placed on the shelf next to the first one. She turned toward Leopold, her eyebrows arched in demand.

"Tomorrow night."

CHAPTER 22
FRIEND OR FOE

With permission from her parents to see a movie after dinner (a lie), Agatha and Tobie picked up Leopold and headed to the Benford-O'Malley Funeral Home on Howard Avenue. Agatha's stomach pulsed with nerves and nausea, and she tried to swallow away the saliva flooding her mouth. Lucius Nikolai was not the most pleasant, and Agatha was still trying to decide if he were friend or foe. Tonight, he'd need to be friend.

Tobie parked the truck in a lot behind Benford-O'Malley Funeral Home. It wasn't midnight, but the funeral home was closed, and it would arouse suspicion with a vehicle in their empty parking lot. Luckily, where they parked had other cars.

"This is silly," Tobie said as he turned off the ignition. "That's all I'm going to say." He pulled a book and his glasses from the truck's console.

"So how long does it take to use your third eye, Agatha? Asking for a friend."

Agatha stuck her tongue out at Tobie and exited the truck. "Don't leave us."

"Wouldn't dream of it," Tobie said, finding the dog-eared place in his book, his eyeglasses making him look like a more handsome Harry Potter and less handsome Tom Cruise.

She slammed the truck's door and looked at Leopold, "You're going inside this time." She handed him Aunt Letty's little book. "Put this in your backpack."

Leopold started to protest, but Agatha was already at the funeral home's rear, tugging at the same window she'd slipped through months ago. It was open. Lucius Nikolai apparently knew things.

She motioned for Leopold to follow her as her body disappeared through the opening. He hesitated for a moment, ultimately deciding to slip through behind Agatha. He tucked a wisp of his brown hair behind his ear several times in a row, something Agatha hadn't seen him do in a long time. She knew he was nervous.

Leopold clicked on a flashlight he retrieved from his backpack, illuminating a small room Agatha found to be exactly as her last visit. Two armchairs in front of a large brown desk were the only pieces of furniture comprising the meeting room for mourners in the first stages of funeral preparation. She proceeded to the door, pulling it open and seeing the same long hallway with green velvet carpet, yellow wallpaper with green flowers, and brass lanterns jutting out from the wall, none of them alight. Several portraits with bronze placards beneath decorated the wall. Agatha's eyes rested on the nearest one. It looked recent and bore the name Bernard Benford. Current funeral directors. She searched for a few moments looking for Lucius Nikolai's portrait but didn't find it.

Agatha removed her shoes, motioning for Leopold to do the same. He clicked his flashlight off, and they both tiptoed out into the hallway.

The funeral home felt unusually cold, and the February air tickled her neck and inched its way into the collar of her jacket where her small body attempted to shiver it off. Leopold's fingers ran along the ridges in the wallpaper until the wall ended, delivering them both into the empty waiting room area with the fireplace where Agatha had last talked with Mr. Lucius Nikolai.

The room was still, and Agatha wasn't sure what to do. On her prior visit, Nikolai was already seated by the fireplace and had beckoned her toward the empty chair adjacent to him. This time, he was nowhere to be found. Perhaps it was too early. She checked her watch. Eight fifty.

Leopold leaned to Agatha's ear. "Does he only come out at midnight or something?"

"I don't know," she whispered out of the corner of her mouth.

Leopold started to turn around. "Welp, I guess he's not here. I'm going to—"

"No, you don't," Agatha interrupted him, leading him onto the red rug in front of the fireplace where the two wingback velvet chairs sat. "Sit," she whispered, pointing to the floor while she took a seat in one of the chairs.

Leopold protested. "Why do I have to sit on the floor when that chair is empty?"

"Because he's going to sit in that one." Agatha shivered again, wishing the fireplace were lit, even if that meant having a discussion with Nikolai again. Leopold sat.

"Lucius?" she said aloud but got no response.

"I think it's too early," Leopold said. He clicked on his flashlight again. "Have you ever been down that hallway?" He pointed behind the chair where Agatha sat.

"No."

"I'm going to look," he said, starting to get up. He tiptoed past Agatha, shining his light into the one open room behind her. "I think it's a kitchen. You think they have any food?"

"Gross, Leopold," she whispered loudly. "Don't eat anything. And turn your flashlight off."

He clicked the flashlight off as they both heard a door slam somewhere in the building. "Hide!" she said, squatting behind the large velvet chair. Leopold ducked into the kitchen and placed himself behind the door, holding his breath.

Agatha crawled to a large fake plant left of the fireplace and positioned herself behind its ceramic pot. The large green leaves provided camouflage, and she peered between two of them.

An older man entered the room, his cell phone to his ear. He tossed his keys onto one of the small buffet tables near the funeral home's entrance. He was short, balding, and probably hadn't spent too many days hungry, Agatha thought. The pants of his suit were several inches too short, and the jacket appeared too tight, the cuffs riding well above his wrists. A roll of neck fat flopped over his shirt's collar. He walked on the sides of his shoes, his waddle causing the fabric of his suit pants to sing a rhyming song. *Whish, whoosh, swish, swoosh.*

"Yes, honey. I just forgot something here at work. I won't be long." He paused a few feet from Agatha, facing away from her, one meaty fist on his hip. "Yes, yes, I know you're tired. So am I. I'll be quick. Need to make sure I shut the door to *the room*. I had a feeling I didn't. Can't have the dead walking around, now, can we?" A high-pitched little giggle exited his mouth followed by a snort. "Yes, love you too."

Agatha cringed. 'The room' must be where they kept the bodies.

The man hung up, pulled a peppermint out of his pocket, and popped it between two eager, plump lips. He licked the stickiness off several fingers and started to hum a tune as he continued down the hallway, thankfully passing the kitchen without entering. Leopold was safe. For now.

Agatha stayed perfectly still behind the plant for a few moments, the dust on its leaves tingling the insides of her nostrils, until she suddenly became aware of a solid presence to her right, the cold breath hitting her neck in an icy hiss. From the corner of her eye, a face leaned near her cheek, its forked tongue flicking its words toward her as they scented the air with a stench.

"Well hello, Agatha Anxious."

CHAPTER 23
THE SHAPESHIFTER

Lucius Nikolai backed away from Agatha and sat in the same velvet chair as last time. “Lovely, isn’t he?” His eyes darted down the hall toward the man she’d just seen moments prior.

Agatha continued to crouch.

“Now, you know it’s rude to not have a seat, don’t you?” Lucius puffed out his bottom lip and pretended to be sad.

Agatha did as he requested, her stockinged feet gliding her over to the remaining chair, where she sat, gently, on the edge. “What...what if the man comes back?”

“I’ll know before he does.” He straightened his cuffs, and Agatha took notice of his attire. The black waistcoat over the same stiff white collared shirt, black pants and Converse shoes.

“How will you know?” she whispered.

Nikolai crossed his hands in his lap, ten long grey, spidery fingers intertwining themselves like pieces of a macabre puzzle. “Because I know everything.” He held up a bony hand and snapped his fingers. “But frankly, you can hear him coming a mile away with that walk of his.”

“Who is he?”

“The present funeral director and owner, Bernard Benford.” Nikolai smiled, the corner of his forked tongue catching between two teeth on the side. “He goes by Bernie. Bernie Benford. A ridiculous name for a ridiculous little man.” His lips spread wide, slowly, like two theatre curtains announcing the start of a play. Nikolai cocked his head to the side and blinked, both sets of eyelids momentarily covering his solid black eyes. “So, what can I do for you, Agatha?”

Agatha turned her head to the side but kept her eyes on Nikolai. “Leopold!” she whispered loudly.

“Yes! Mr. Panic. Of course, please come join us, good sir.” Nikolai called out.

“What?”

“Come out here.”

“No way, that dude is still down the hallway,” Leopold said, referring to Mr. Benford. He was trying to keep his voice to a whisper.

“I know, but—” Agatha stopped. Leopold hadn’t wanted to come in the first place, and now he was avoiding Nikolai altogether. She decided to proceed without him. She didn’t have all night.

Agatha looked down at her hands in her lap. “A taste for a truth, I suppose?”

Nikolai crossed his legs, rested both arms on the sides of the chair and nodded.

"How many questions do I get? You tried to trick me last time."

Nikolai let out a dusty laugh, a rattling, mucus-y wheeze inside his chest. "Me? I've never tried to trick a soul!" He coughed a couple of times, dotting his mouth with a white handkerchief from his waistcoat. "Not anyone who didn't deserve it, I mean."

Agatha was undeterred. "How many questions do I get?" she repeated.

Nikolai stared for a moment at her, his black eyes suddenly serious. "Two."

Agatha narrowed her eyes at him in return. "That's less than last time."

Nikolai shrugged, a quiet smirk in the corner of his mouth, upturned and arrogant, as if saying "And?"

Agatha thought for a moment, categorizing her multiple questions according to importance. All seemed to be important.

Nikolai produced the small glass vial from his pocket and used his sharp teeth to uncork the lid, their points grasping it like a venus flytrap. She held out her hand and looked away, feeling the quick sting of his jagged fingernails on her skin. A wet warmth pooled on the pad of her ring finger and dripped down the side. He squeezed for several seconds, and she imagined her blood dripping into the little vial, thick and murky. Nikolai kept squeezing, and she finally looked. Instead of several prick marks like last time, he'd sliced the tip of her finger right across the ridges forming her fingerprint.

"Hey!" she started to protest, and he squeezed harder until she snatched her hand back.

Nikolai stood and retreated to the corner by the fireplace, partially hidden in darkness. He turned his back to her and held the vial up to his lips. Agatha couldn't see what he was doing, but she didn't need to. The memory of his snakelike tongue creeping and curving into the bottle and tasting her blood made her head pulse with pain. She felt dizzy again and scooted back into the chair, fully relaxing her body into its velvet fabric. Her head lolled left and right, and her eyelids flitted closed. She struggled to keep them open, but they were heavy, and her vision was out of focus. She knew this to be the repercussions of his finger prick, and she took in a deep breath, filling her lungs with air to ward off the anxiety.

Seconds or minutes or hours passed—Agatha wasn't quite sure—and she opened her eyes to find Nikolai seated again across from her, his fingers interlaced at his chin. He smiled like a giddy schoolgirl.

"I'm ready when you are, Agatha Anxious. I don't have all night." He barked out a laugh at his own comment. "Nevermind, yes, I do. I have all night every night." He pointed at her. "But you don't."

"Leopold!" Agatha whispered again. "Get in here."

This time Leopold did as he was told, peering like a child down the hallway in the middle of the night, afraid to go to the bathroom because of the monsters lurking in the darkness. He stepped into the room, and Agatha pointed to the floor next to her chair since she and Nikolai were occupying the chairs.

"Sit here for a few minutes."

"Again?" Leopold pointed to the red rug. "Why do I have to sit on the floor when—"

"Just do it, please," she said, watching Nikolai. Leopold lowered himself to the floor and crossed his legs, looking back down the hallway for Bernard Benford.

Agatha cleared her throat. "I need to know how to get rid of a Deceiver."

Nikolai's eyebrows arched in an exaggerated surprise, and Agatha wondered if he already knew. "A Deceiver?"

She nodded.

"Are you sure it's a Deceiver?"

She nodded again. "I think so."

"Do you know what a Deceiver is, Agatha?"

"I think so," she repeated. "I want to ask, but I don't want that to count as one of my questions."

"You tell me what you think it is, and I'll confirm or not."

"And it won't count?" Agatha asked, being specific. She didn't want to get robbed of any of her questions.

Nikolai shook his head, his black eyes remained open and wide. "No."

"My friend Tippy used a book to summon her dead brother. Her dead brother, Henry, happens to be my childhood imaginary friend. Well, I thought he was imaginary. I guess he really wasn't. He was a real person. Anyway, I think she summoned something else. Something that looks and acts like her brother, but the mean version." Agatha paused to bite a hangnail that had snagged on her dress. "The evil version."

Nikolai nodded. "Good, good."

"I saw his face turn into Blanche Caillavet's face. That's what made me realize there were two versions."

Nikolai's face fell, and Agatha perceived a strange irritation. His voiced edged with annoyance. "Oh really?"

"Yes. I...I think she must be somehow controlling it. Or maybe that's HER. I don't know."

"You are mostly correct. A Deceiver is a copy of someone or something. I like to call them mimics or shapeshifters if you will. It's a replica. One which intends to do harm, create conflict, spread chaos and confusion."

Agatha huffed. "Well, it's doing all of that. But what is it doing to

Big? My imaginary friend, I mean. It's doing something to him. What, exactly?"

Nikolai narrowed his eyes, his mouth ajar and dripping with deception. "Is this your first question?"

Agatha nodded. "Yes." She looked over at Leopold whose eyes were wild. "What?" she mouthed.

Leopold scooted backwards toward the wall across from the fireplace, his eyes darting back and forth between Agatha's chair and Nikolai's.

Nikolai stared at Leopold for a few moments, amused. Then he stood and walked to the mantle. He clapped his hands and just like last time, the logs were alight with fire and flame.

"What?" she mouthed again to Leopold.

Leopold shook his head and pointed to Nikolai's chair. Agatha didn't understand.

Nikolai giggled. "Well, isn't this a surprise."

"What is a surprise?" Agatha had the feeling he was mocking her.

Another giggle. "Nevermind. Things just got a bit more interesting," Nikolai said, smiling in Leopold's direction. "We'll get to that momentarily. Regarding your question, the simplest answer I can give you, Agatha, is that Deceivers eventually kill whomever they're mimicking."

"But Big is already dead."

"Mm-hmm," Nikolai said, now fiddling with one of his fingers, disinterested.

"And no, that's not another question. I'm thinking out loud."

"It doesn't matter if he's already dead," Nikolai said finally, taking a seat again. "The longer a Deceiver is present, the longer your friend—Big? —won't be able to rest. That's what the dead do, isn't it? Rest?

And they can't rest, the further away from the grave they become, so to speak."

"Further away?"

Nikolai dusted something off his shirt. "Not 'further away' literally. I mean to say the more Big's ghost will be destined to roam the earth aimlessly. No rest. No solace. No salvation. Forever."

"The Deceiver woke him up," Agatha said.

"Yes."

"And he wants to be back in his grave. Resting."

"Yes."

"Ok, how do I get rid of a Deceiver? THAT's my second question."

Nikolai's head shot up and he smiled, as if finally ridding himself of a long-held secret. "You don't."

"What?"

"You don't. To be more precise, *you* can't, Agatha." Nikolai pointed a thin finger toward Leopold. "But he can."

"Leopold?" She looked at him in amazement. "How?"

Nikolai smirked. "If I answered that, I'd be giving you a third question. But he can tell you himself. He's been doing a lot of research lately, haven't you, Mr. Panic?"

Agatha stared at Leopold who still cowered against the wall. He'd pulled his knees to his chest and buried almost all his face into his arms. Only his eyes were still visible, staring in Nikolai's direction.

"Leopold?"

Leopold darted his green eyes toward Agatha.

"What is it?" she asked.

Leopold slowly lifted his chin away from his arms and pointed toward Nikolai's chair. Agatha saw his hand was shaking. "Is he sitting there?"

"Of course, he is. We've been having a whole conversation. Haven't you heard it? About Deceivers."

Leopold stared at the fireplace, the dancing yellow and orange of the flames reflected in his pupils. He didn't blink. His face fell with a realization and his shoulders slumped. "I've heard you, Agatha. But only you. I can't see Lucius Nikolai."

CHAPTER 24
DAMAGED

Agatha sprung from her chair and backed away from Nikolai, joining Leopold near the wall. "Why can't he see you?" she said demanded, loudly.

"Hello?" said a voice down the hallway. Mr. Benford.

Agatha grabbed Leopold's wrist and drug him behind the plant with her.

"Is someone out here?"

Agatha heard the swish swoosh of his pants long before she saw him. He paused at the entrance to the kitchen, dialing a number on his cell phone. "Hey hon, I'm leaving. Everything's locked up. No wild parties to break up here." He snorted and entered the kitchen.

Agatha heard the refrigerator door open and the crinkling of a paper bag. He returned to the waiting room, again only a few feet away from her, hurriedly stuffing half a sandwich in his mouth as he continued to talk. A piece of deli meat dangled from his lip which he jammed into his mouth with a sausage thumb. "Time to come home, I'm starting to hear voices around here." He snorted again. He used the same thumb to scratch the inside of a nostril, the whole tip of his finger disappearing into his nose.

Nikolai remained seated in his chair and snickered. "Ah, Bernie Benford. Such a Biloxi treasure."

Mr. Benford, oblivious to the presence of Lucius Nikolai, grabbed his keys and departed down the hallway. Agatha didn't move until she heard a door close on the other side of the building.

"This does NOT count as a question. Why can't Leopold see you?" She stood in front of the fireplace, deciding she didn't want to sit any longer.

Leopold remained behind the plant.

"I suspect he knows why," Nikolai's gaze was hard and cold, but something else was there too. Amusement, Agatha saw. As usual, he was delighted in whatever misery or misfortune perplexed her. Delighted she'd come. Delighted she had questions that needed answering. Delighted in the power her Perceiver blood offered him, but not aligned or loyal to her in any way.

Perceiver blood, she thought. The reason he wanted her to come but didn't necessarily want to help her. At that moment, Agatha was quite certain she'd found Mr. Lucius Nikolai's weakness. He couldn't do without it. He *required* it.

"Two more questions. A taste for a truth." Nikolai's second set of eyelids washed over his eyes, a jellylike substance filling his sockets. His expression softened, and he smiled. He was pleased.

Agatha pointed to Leopold. "Take his blood this time."

Nikolai scooted away in his chair, repulsed. "No. Yours."

"Why? He's a Perceiver too."

"He's..." Nikolia looked away from Leopold, "...damaged."

Agatha's heart flipped a couple beats, and a cozy feeling of triumph flooded her veins. She'd gotten Nikolai to answer a question without having to ask one.

Leopold slowly appeared from behind the plant and stood there, unsure what to do. "What is he saying?"

Agatha stared at Nikolai. "He is saying your blood is no good. You also can't see him even though you're a Perceiver and you saw him last time. All of that can only mean one thing."

Leopold nodded. "The Deceiver."

"Yes, I think so."

"Because I touched it," Leopold continued, dazed with the discovery. "Are my powers gone forever? Ask him."

"I don't get another question," Agatha said.

"Smart boy," Nikolai said at last. He lowered his head and peered at Agatha wickedly underneath the bone that protruded over where his eyebrows should've been. He sneered in her direction, delighting again in Agatha's confusion. "A Perceiver cannot touch a Deceiver."

Agatha thrust her hand in Nikolai's direction, her open palm causing him to salivate. "Two more questions. Hurry."

The same groggy feeling washed over her, and Agatha wasn't sure how much time had passed by the time she came to. She found herself sitting on the floor by the fireplace, Leopold next to her. He was so close, she felt the fear emanating off him.

"I'm sorry," she whispered.

"For what?"

"For leaving you alone for a few minutes. I don't know what happens, but I'm sort of out of it for a bit."

"It's ok," Leopold said, making no move to scoot away from her. "I can't see him anyway, remember? So, I can't be afraid, really." He attempted a smile.

But he was afraid, and Agatha knew it. She looked at Nikolai, who was pacing between the two chairs, his hands in his pockets. She wondered what he'd been like in life as the undertaker at the funeral home. Pleasant? Friendly? Obviously, his business was a success, so he couldn't have been too creepy, although weren't *all* funeral homes and their employees somewhat creepy?

Agatha tugged at the zipper on Leopold's backpack, which was still around his shoulders. She retrieved Aunt Letty's book and held it up to Nikolai. "There was an epilogue about Deceivers, and the Deceiver tore it out."

Leopold elbowed Agatha.

She cleared her throat. "Or...someone did." She still couldn't bring herself to consider Dorian doing something so nefarious.

"Yes?" Nikolai wasn't the least bit interested, though he'd stopped his pacing.

"I want to know what the epilogue said."

Nikolai threw his head back and laughed. Agatha saw straight into the back of his mouth. Even his phlegm was black. "How should I know what that chapter said? I didn't write the book."

"You said you know everything."

Nikolai smirked. "Indeed, I did, but no, I don't know what the epilogue of your pathetic little book said."

Agatha huffed. For the moment, she was no longer concerned about the Deceiver. Tippy was the one who caused it, she was the one who could deal with it. "How does Leopold get his powers back? That's my first question."

Immediately, Agatha felt a pit of regret form in her belly. She knew Tippy was desperate to get rid of the Deceiver. Not only that, but Big was too. His eternal fate rested solely on the demise of the Deceiver. And only then would he be at peace and Agatha get her second shard of the mirror glass. Everything was a domino effect, each tiny piece relying on the piece before it for success.

She put her head in her hands, and Leopold put his arm around her shoulders. His gesture didn't feel strange or weird or out of place. For the first time, the touch of a boy didn't make her feel awkward or make her insides a topsy turvy mixture of innards and guts. She welcomed it. It was genuine. He was concerned too. Currently, he was the only person in the whole world who understood, and now he'd lost the one thing that aligned himself with Agatha Anxious: his Perceiver abilities.

Nikolai squatted in front of them both with ease, as if his knees were rubber, bending precisely as he instructed them to do with no complaining indicative of a man his age. This time he was serious. "The Deceiver is darkness, Agatha. And because of his touch, the darkness has attached itself to Leopold. He is the only one who can do something about it. Precisely *what* is to be done is up to Leopold." He looked at Leopold and smiled. "He's a smart young man. I'm sure he'll figure it out. In fact, Agatha, the answers are all around you. Right in front of you, really. You just have to look."

With nothing more to say, Nikolai got comfortable in his chair.

Agatha stood up, indignant. "That's your answer? That Leopold will figure it out himself?"

"I gave you an answer. You're not listening."

"What was the answer?" she demanded.

"What did he say?" Leopold was standing now too.

"He said the Deceiver was darkness. And the darkness was attached to you, and you're the only one who can figure out how to get rid of the darkness. Right?" she stared at Nikolai. "Isn't that what you said."

Nikolai nodded, pleased. "You were listening."

Agatha grabbed Leopold's hand. "Come on, we're leaving."

"So soon?" Nikolai feigned surprise. "But you have one more question! Oh nevermind, I'll add it on to next time."

They rushed down the hallway, scooping up their shoes in the meeting room, and Agatha pointed to the window, directing Leopold to exit. She popped her head back into the hallway. "No, Mr. Nikolai. I know how important my blood is to you, and I've decided you need me far more than I need you. I don't need another question because I won't be back." With that, she crawled through the window not waiting for his reply.

Nikolai's face fell and he stood, his angry exhales the only sound in the silent funeral home. He extinguished the fire with a flick of his hand, and he gripped the mantle with his fingers, the brown nails digging into the wood. He gritted his teeth, grinding the hundreds of points together until a few of them broke into pieces, leaving jagged pieces jutting from his black gums.

"Oh yes you will," he seethed.

CHAPTER 25
THE CREATURE IN THE WINDOW

Agatha and Leopold ran wildly toward Tobie's truck where she beat her hands against the passenger window until he unlocked the door.

"Good Lord, Agatha. You scared me," Tobie said, annoyed. His eyes were slit, and his cheeks were rosy. Agatha could tell he'd been sleeping.

"Drive us home." She was out of breath, though the run was short. Her anxiety had been awakened at her boldness and now had her lungs in a vice grip. She struggled to get a deep breath.

Tobie looked at the funeral home and narrowed his eyes. "Ok, what in the heck just happened in there? I mean it. What happened?"

Agatha was silent. Leopold stared out the window, completely lost in a thought, and Agatha wasn't sure he'd even heard Tobie. He was his own planet, rotating and floating on its own, aimlessly in a faraway galaxy.

Tobie stared at the two large slits on her ring finger, dried blood covering the entire tip. "What happened?" He pouted and threw her the keys. "Nevermind, I'm going in there."

"Wait, what?" Agatha's breaths were now coming out in short little rasps. "What?"

"This is ridiculous. I'm going in there."

"Wait here," she told Leopold, who didn't budge. She climbed past the steering wheel and followed Tobie out the driver's side door. "Tobie, stop!" Embarrassment rushed up her neck and into her cheeks at the sound of the desperation in her voice. What did it matter if Tobie went into the funeral home? He'd find nothing. He'd see nothing. And he'd be more inclined than ever to think Agatha was an idiot. What did that matter? Did she care? This was her mission, not Tobie's.

"I saw which window you crawled through." He stopped and put a finger to his lips. "Or wait, maybe I'll knock on the front door. Will a gremlin answer it?" He rounded the corner toward the funeral home's front, kicking at a few clumps of grass out of his way.

Agatha managed to catch up with him, her short legs in a jog to keep up with his long strides. She checked her watch. It was nearing ten. "We should get home. Our movie would be over soon." Tobie didn't respond. "What are you even going to do in there?"

Tobie was at the front door now. "There's no such thing as ghosts, Agatha. I'm about to show you there's not one living thing in this place right now." He raised his hand to knock.

"I didn't say there was anything *living* in there."

Tobie snickered. "Ok, Agatha." He rapped three times on the door, hard and slow. He leaned toward Agatha, asking out of the side of his mouth with a grin, "And whom should I ask for once I get inside? Jimi Hendrix?"

"Who?"

Tobie shook his head and made a tsk tsk noise with his tongue. "Glory be, Agatha. I'm not sure if I'm more surprised you believe in ghosts or that you don't know who that is." He knocked twice more. Still nothing.

He raised his eyebrows at Agatha and smiled. "See? No ghosts tonight." He started back toward the truck, stuffing his hands in the pockets of his jacket. "Or any night for that matter."

He opened the door for Agatha, who crawled in, thankful for the warmth of the truck, the presence of Leopold, and the knowledge that the night was almost over. She scooted close to Leopold and laid her head on his shoulder. He made no move to indicate he knew she was there, still lost in his thoughts. She closed her eyes.

Tobie slid in beside her and buckled his seatbelt before starting the truck. He looked over at Agatha and shook his head. A small grunt escaped his lips. "Shoulda gone in through there," he said under his breath, his eyes finding their way over to the funeral home and the building's far right window, which was still slightly ajar after Agatha and Leopold's hurried exit. "Maybe I would've seen Jimi Hen—"

The words caught in his throat as a grey hand pulled the window closed, the figure purposely standing in full view of October Anxious. A black waist coast, black pants, and long thin limbs. Its greyish skin stretched exaggeratedly over its bony face, the black eyes leaning near the pane of glass to stare directly at Tobie.

Tobie held his breath as he fumbled in the darkness to find the gearshift, throwing the truck into drive and peeling out of the parking lot. He kept his eyes on the creature as it pressed both of its spidery hands against the window's glass, exposing hundreds of sharp points in its mouth, and smiled.

CHAPTER 26
YES, FATHER

Nikolai spat into his hand, several pieces of his broken teeth falling into his grey palm. He returned to the mantle and threw them toward the fireplace, the white pieces disappearing into thin air as they left his fingers. Within moments, the sharp edges in his mouth were whole again, smooth and polished, too numerous to count.

"You gave yourself away," he said aloud, seething. "She would've never known there were two of them without you doing so. I taught you better."

There was no response.

"I know you're there, whether you respond or not. Do you forget that I am part of you, dearest?" He hissed the last word.

Nikolai curled his long fingers into fists and stuffed them into his pockets, thinking. "You must be careful. The boy has given you his power, but it can quite easily be taken away. Now is not the time to be careless. Agatha Anxious is struggling with what to do, and Mr. Panic is the only hope. I'm not sure he's as smart as she is, which for us is...." Nikolai smiled, pressing his thin lips together into a wide half circle, "... fortunate. Regardless, be careful."

He turned to face the empty sitting room, fully aware his companion was present. "Answer me!" he shouted.

From the hallway to Nikolai's left was the response. A brass lantern jutting out from the wall, flickered twice and then went dark. The funeral home was silent except for the husky whisper of an angry woman.

"Yes, father."

CHAPTER 27
I'VE BEEN SEEING THINGS

Upon her return to school on Friday, Agatha was disappointed to find Mr. Barone had a substitute for her first period History class. He was her favorite teacher, and she looked forward to each morning's eclectic outfit. She was doubly disappointed to find Mrs. Wright *didn't* have a substitute, and she gruffly reminded the class of their Black History Icon reports due Monday.

Agatha hadn't seen Leopold all day, which was highly unusual. Leopold never missed school. She did, however, catch a glimpse of Tippy during lunch, and she looked more awful than she had a few days prior at the mask shop. The bags under her eyes had gotten darker, her hair was unkempt and unwashed, her normally luminous skin appeared sallow. Agatha felt like a complete failure.

She hadn't rid her friend of the Deceiver. She hadn't helped Big return to his grave. In the last week, she hadn't done much at all, really. No steps forward. In each case, every effort seemed to be a step backwards. Retrieving the book from Tippy, the morgue visit, the pier fiasco, the evening with Nikolai. Agatha shuddered. She wondered what his response was to her last statement before diving through the window.

Tippy caught Agatha at her locker at the end of the day.

"I need to talk to you," she said, staring at the Black History Month posters where Martin Luther King, Jr., was informing her only light could drive out darkness and Sojourner Truth proclaimed to feel safe in the midst of her enemies.

"Ok," Agatha said, hesitant. She looked around, noticing all the bodies smushed together at their lockers, the hallway filled with hand holding and hoots and hollers signaling the end of the school day and the weekend's beginning. "Walk with me."

They walked through the school's front doors, finding a quieter place in the shade of an old oak tree out front. Agatha kept watch for Tobie's truck.

"I've...I've been seeing things," Tippy's shoulders were shaking.

"Big?"

She shook her head emphatically. "No. Something different. Completely different." She blew out a breath, trying to keep from crying. Agatha waited for her to continue but wasn't sure she wanted her to proceed.

"It's a, um..." she swallowed.

Agatha put her hand on Tippy's arm. "Just say it."

Just then Tobie pulled up and double tapped his horn. He seemed to be in a rush, rolling down the window and waving her on with his hand.

"A what?" Agatha said hurriedly.

"Don't worry about it," Tippy started to walk toward her house on the beach. Agatha grabbed her by the shoulder.

"No, tell me. Hurry."

"A woman. That's what I've been seeing." She popped her knuckles.

Agatha took a couple steps back from Tippy, and she noticed. "What? What's that mean?" Tippy's voice was shaking.

"I, I don't know," was all Agatha could respond. She saw Tobie again waving at her from her periphery. "I will call you. I promise." Agatha broke into a sprint toward the truck, her pulse quickening in her ears.

Tobie drove them home in silence, and Agatha noticed.

"You ok?"

He nodded. "Yeah."

"Really?"

He nodded but didn't respond.

"Are you mad about last night?"

"Mad?" He half smiled. "Now when have you seen me mad, Agatha?"

She shrugged. "Never."

"I don't get mad. And no, I'm not mad about last night. What would I have to be mad about?" He cleared his throat, uneasy.

"I dunno."

"That makes two of us," he said, pulling into the driveway of her home. "Now grab your stuff and let's go. We gotta get to the shop and then I want to get to mom's house before you ask me to drive you to some funeral home or empty hospital again. Maybe you'll ask me to spend the night in the cemetery in somebody's crypt next time or something. Anyway, not how I planned on spending my weekend. Or my life."

Agatha froze, the truck door half open. "What do you mean grab my stuff?"

"Your parents are doing stuff tonight. Did they not tell you?"

Agatha shook her head. Or did they? Admittedly they might've. Too many things had happened in the past week. Agatha had no room left in her brain for normal, everyday conversations and memories. "I don't know."

"Ok, well, guess what?"

Agatha frowned at Tobie. "My parents are doing stuff tonight." She was in no mood.

Tobie fired his fingers at her like a gun. "Bingo. I guess they wanted a night alone, belated Valentine's stuff, I dunno. And we're staying with mom." He added the last part quickly, as he exited the truck and shut the door.

Agatha whipped her head around to face Tobie. "At Aunt Hattie's house?"

He paused, looking at her through the window. "Well, yeah, I guess if that's what you're still calling it. I kinda call it mom's house."

In her room, Agatha stuffed a small bag with two dresses but avoided packing any pajamas. She threw her blue toothbrush in the bag too, along with some deodorant her mother had recently bought her, insisting she wear it daily. Truthfully, Agatha didn't think she needed it, but it did smell good, even if the label was all pink and boasted a bouquet of roses on the front. Lastly, she reluctantly grabbed Aunt Letty's book, guessing it was time to return it to its owner. It wasn't offering her much assistance, but maybe she could corner Aunt Letty about it.

On her desk, she noticed her mother had laid a brand-new pair of jeans, and Agatha mulled over whether to take them with her or not. *Nah,* she thought. Not yet.

Tobie helped MacBeth into the cab of the truck as Agatha kissed HattieCat on the head, leaving her a large bowl of food and water. She shook her head at the litter box and wondered how Aunt Hattie felt about her new body, new cuisine, new 'bathroom,' new everything. She kissed her twice more, gathering her in her arms and holding her for a few moments before Tobie lightly double-tapped the horn from the driveway.

"I love you, Auntie," she whispered into the cat's scruff.

The hours at the shop were boring, but Aunt Letty allowed Agatha to sit behind the cash register, showing her a few of the buttons. She was thankful not to have to dust anything today, especially any of the booths of Red Rum Row.

"Did Leopold call to say he wasn't coming today?" she asked Aunt Letty as she popped the money drawer open, fiddling with a few of the coins before closing it.

"As a matter of fact, he did."

"He did?"

"Yes, said he wasn't feeling well but had to work on school report at the library." Aunt Letty pushed dark thick black glasses up to the top of her head, her short blonde hair looking wild behind her ears. A black turtleneck sweater sat just beneath her chin, paired with a black lace skirt. To her ankles, of course.

"Oh."

"Why?"

"He wasn't at school today."

"Well, sounds about right, then." She stared at Agatha for a few moments. "Why do you look so concerned?"

Agatha shrugged. She wasn't going to tell her the truth. "He's just never sick. That's all."

At closing time, Aunt Letty turned off all the lights, locked all of Aunt Hattie's locks, and pulled the back door closed behind them, the large mirror still affixed to the outside of it. Aunt Letty hadn't changed a thing, and Agatha wondered if her house would be the same way, too. She couldn't decide if she hoped it was or hoped it wasn't.

The twenty-five-minute drive to Aunt Hattie's house was in silence. Tobie staring intently out the windshield as if he weren't really focused on the road.

"What are you thinking about?" Agatha finally asked him. "Like, right this minute. What?"

"Um, nothing really. School." He seemed caught off guard, and she suspected he was lying but said no more.

She opened her phone, deciding to text Tippy on the way.

Hey. She waited a few minutes until the reply came.

Hey.

I can't call, but I can text. Tell me what you saw.

There was a long pause while it seemed Tippy was deciding what to say. Agatha waited a full five minutes but there was nothing from Tippy. She closed her phone and sighed.

Tobie pulled into the driveway. Agatha kept her eyes in her lap, not ready to look at the house just yet. He hooked the leash onto MacBeth and headed to the front porch. "Come inside when you're ready," he called to her, and she appreciated not having to explain herself.

Agatha listened to the night noises. Crickets, the croaking of frogs, the nocturnal animals announcing the commencing of the night. The hum of a streetlamp near the road played a low chord in the distance, and Agatha looked up at the house.

Her gaze was greeted with the inviting little brown abode that was once Aunt Hattie's. Three white cats curled themselves around each other on the porch, delighting in each other's warmth. Agatha willed her legs to carry her to the front porch where she reluctantly grasped the knob of the front door. It felt cold in her palm, indicative of the emptiness that awaited her on the other side of the door. She turned it and entered.

CHAPTER 28
SWEET SADNESS

The sweet smell of Aunt Hattie hit Agatha as soon as she entered her house, the delicious, musky scent finding its way into her nostrils and conjuring up old memories as if her nose were directly connected to her heart. Each electrical beat fired off a new something to be sad about: her aunt's husky laugh, the way the silver braids of her hair brushed her back, the soft skin of her bony hands, the silence of a house without Aunt Hattie.

Moving from room to room, Agatha saw ordinary objects that became weapons, stabbing her in methodical waves of grief. Aunt Hattie's blue glasses on the end table by the couch, unworn in months. Her favorite coffee cup by the sink. An opened bag of popcorn kernels on the counter by the microwave. One of her multicolored, ruffled skirts hanging in the laundry room, long dry but not put away. Aunt Letty had kept everything the same. Everything. Which was both pleasing and terrifying to Agatha. Aunt Hattie's house had become an armory of objects meant to emotionally destroy her.

Tobie made himself at home on the couch and smiled sadly in her direction, again somehow knowing things without saying them. He couldn't empathize, though. He hadn't known Aunt Hattie, really, but he could somewhat understand. He flipped through the channels on the television, the stick of a sucker protruding from his mouth.

"Am I in the back room?" Agatha asked Aunt Letty, who was preparing a bowl of milk for the porch cats.

She nodded. "That's Tobie's room when he stays here, but he'll sleep on the couch this weekend."

Agatha heard the front door open as she proceeded down the hallway, Aunt Letty's voice trailing off as she said something to the cats. She slowly pushed open the door to Aunt Hattie's room, the amber glow of the room enveloping her as she entered. The same dark grey walls, twin bed, and grey nightstand. Numerous mirrors lining the walls. Black and white family portraits. Aunt Hattie's books on the nightstand had now been replaced with several boxes of puzzles. Agatha looked at the top box without touching it. A beach scene. Aunt Letty must like puzzles.

Next to the boxes sat a framed little photograph of two girls sitting on the stump of a tree. One blonde, one brunette. Agatha swallowed away a small lump that formed in her throat. The chocolate chip cookie brown eyes, quirky smile, and olive skin were a dead giveaway. Aunt Hattie and Aunt Letty were hugging, their cheeks pressed tightly together, wide, toothy grins on both of their faces. Agatha swallowed again.

She tiptoed down the hallway to the purple bedroom and yanked the cord on one of the beaded lamps on the nightstand. She placed her small bag on the floor by the closet, being careful to keep a distance from the brown wardrobe in the corner. It wore its usual frown, the two large front doors tightly closed, the iron knobs staring at her like judging eyes. This room had no air or inkling of a teenage boy like Tobie staying in it, but that made sense. He practically lived with Agatha.

"Maybe you and Tobie can help me move that thing."

Agatha jumped. She didn't know Aunt Letty had been watching her. Had she seen her snooping in her room?

"That?" Agatha pointed toward the wardrobe.

"Yes. I'm going to put it in my bedroom. Someday. But it's heavy. Maybe we can slide it."

Agatha nodded, mentally noting to make it her mission *not* to remind Aunt Letty about moving the wardrobe. No way was she touching that thing. Tobie could help her. He could probably move it by himself. *Poor Tobie.*

"I'm making tacos. They'll be ready in about thirty minutes," Aunt Letty said, heading toward the kitchen.

Agatha opened the nightstand and found, as she'd suspected, one of her nightgowns, folded just like Aunt Hattie would've folded it. She felt another ripple of grief as she touched the cotton of the nightdress, ultimately closing the drawer without putting it on. Aunt Hattie had a particular way of folding clothes, rolling them up in little tubes so you could see each item in a drawer. Seven, ten or twelve perfect cylindrical shirts or skirts or pajama tops were usually displayed neatly in her own drawers. Agatha decided she'd sleep in her clothes. She wanted to keep that one nightdress exactly as it was, the last hands to have folded it being Aunt Hattie's.

She heard the grease popping from the kitchen as Tobie poked his head in the door.

"Tacos!" he said and smiled. "I'm guessing you've never had mom's tacos."

Agatha shook her head.

"They're the best you'll ever taste. She hand-fries all the flour tortillas, too. Nice and crispy." He lowered his voice. "That's the secret. No corn tortillas. Flour." He looked her up and down for a moment. "You alright?"

"Yeah," Agatha said.

"There's no alien poster in here. I think you just might survive the night. Maybe." He winked and disappeared.

She opened her phone to check if Tippy had responded and saw a few messages. A few pumps of adrenaline ran through her heart as she opened the texts.

Boi soiuoibuie boisoos eoioigboisue.

Boiosf boisg onrdos boosidbsodiv

Boisbosi bsosdobidsiosdo!

Boosbos bodiosibosiiee!!!!

Agatha furrowed her brow. She began typing.

What? I don't understand.

Her phone immediately lit up with a phone call from Tippy. She answered. "Hey, I can't read what you—"

Tippy's hurried voice came through in a hushed whisper. "I'm trying to text you and it won't go through. I don't know why!" She sounded frantic.

"Ok, ok. What are you trying to type?" said Agatha.

"A woman!" Tippy bellowed into the phone in between quick breaths. Her last words were hauntingly clear before Agatha heard the unmistakable click of the phone going dead.

"I think I saw a woman. A woman in white."

CHAPTER 29
J. WILTZ

Tobie was right. The tacos were epic, and Agatha couldn't help but overeat even though her stomach undulated with an enormous amount of worry for Tippy. Had the Deceiver now turned into something else? Blanche? Was it her? She felt nauseous but demanded her stomach hold onto its delicious contents, so she excused herself to the bedroom where she sprawled herself out on the queen-sized bed.

When she opened her eyes, it was dark. Aunt Letty or Tobie must've turned off the lamp. The house was quiet, and Agatha knew it was late. She didn't even realize she'd fallen asleep. She flipped open her phone and saw the time. Quarter to midnight. No more messages or phone calls from Tippy. She decided to text her.

Are you ok? I will figure this out, Tippy. Don't worry. The text wouldn't send. Being out in the country, the service wasn't great at Aunt Hattie's house.

Her bladder notified her of its impatience, but she was scared. The house had a different feel without Aunt Hattie. Was it too quiet? Too still? She peeked into the hallway to see if the television was on. It wasn't. Tobie was asleep before midnight on the weekend?

A small light over the stove was on, though, casting a murky yellow aura down the hallway. Agatha tiptoed toward it. Peering around the corner, she saw Aunt Letty sitting at the small table in the middle of the kitchen, steam rising from a little yellow coffee cup beside her. She was shuffling cards. Agatha cleared her throat as she entered the kitchen, and Aunt Letty looked up.

"Can't sleep?" she managed a small smile in the corner of her mouth, one side of her thin lips turned upward.

"I did sleep but didn't mean to."

Aunt Letty nodded, uttering something like "Mmm" before returning to her cards, which were now placed in seven columns of Solitaire. "You can sit if you'd like." She placed a jack on top of a queen followed by a ten on top of the jack.

Agatha slid into one of the small chairs at the kitchen table, her eyes on Aunt Letty's game while she continued to play, saying nothing. Every now and then, her aunt would look up from the cards, studying her for a few moments and then return to her game.

After a while, Aunt Letty broke the silence. "What would you like to say?" Agatha looked up. "Me? Oh, um, nothing. I'm, I'm just watching you play." She was a terrible liar.

Aunt Letty took a sip from her coffee cup, slurping loudly, her eyes on Agatha. Tobie snoozed in the living room, his long legs bent awkwardly, a poor attempt at fitting himself on the couch. Agatha bit her lip and returned her aunt's gaze.

"Aunt Letty," she began, taking a moment to choose the proper words, "I miss Aunt Hattie." Agatha's intended question turned into a statement.

Aunt Letty sat back in her chair, turning a few of the cards over in her hands. "Me too." She began gathering all the columns of cards into one neat pile and poured herself another cup of coffee from the coffee maker. Aunt Letty sliced two pieces from an angel food cake on the counter, the numerous crumbs around it indicating she had already enjoyed a piece.

Aunt Letty set them both on the table, and sat down, Agatha taking note of her aunt's pajamas: a collared, long red and black flannel nightdress with large black buttons, black slippers, and a navy robe. She'd never seen Aunt Letty in her pajamas.

Her aunt pushed a piece toward Agatha. "What do you miss most about her?" she asked, her teeth slicing through her piece of the cake, a few crumbs resting on her lip.

Agatha picked at a piece of skin on her thumb. "All of her." It was the first thing that came to mind and more importantly, the absolute truth.

Aunt Letty stopped chewing for a moment and sighed. "That's a good way of putting it. I miss our phone calls. I didn't get to see her much, but we talked a lot. Cooking questions, good books, sometimes we'd sing together. Harriet had such a dark, lovely voice, you know. Honestly though, just nothing at all. Truthfully, I miss talking to her about nothing at all. Those conversations were the best."

Agatha continued to pick until it started to bleed, taking in Aunt Letty's words. "I feel sad about some things I didn't say. Or maybe what I shouldn't have said." She paused, her voice getting quieter. "Or done."

Aunt Letty put her fork down and reached across the table, her firm grip enveloping Agatha's tiny arm. "That's called regret, and you wouldn't be human if you didn't have regrets." She patted Agatha's hand a couple times. "Don't worry. I feel the same way."

Agatha sniffed, trying to stifle the tears she knew were forming at the corners of her eyes. "What do you regret, Aunt Letty?"

"A lot. Too much to say tonight. Just a lot." She managed a small smile.

Agatha stared at her aunt. It was now or never. "Aunt Letty, do you know what a Perceiver is?"

Aunt Letty showed no surprise, confusion, nor shock. "Of course."

Agatha's mouth fell open slightly. She hadn't expected the answer so quickly, and *that* answer.

"Are you one?" Momentum was on Agatha's side, and she didn't want to waste it.

Her aunt shook her head. "No, dear." She took another bite of cake and motioned toward Tobie. "That's why I have him."

Agatha followed her gaze. "What do you mean?"

"Nothing," she said, changing the subject. "Do you not want your cake?"

"Oh, I forgot it was there." Agatha reluctantly took a bite, her stomach still full and expanded from the tacos.

"I know Hattie was a Perceiver, and my guess is you are too."

Agatha nodded, her mouth full of spongy sweetness.

"I figured so. Harriet shared a few things with me over the years, but probably not everything." Aunt Letty finished her last bite of cake, licking two of her fingers before bringing the plate to the sink. "You know, she had a journal." Aunt Letty stared out of the window over the sink, overlooking the backyard.

"What?"

"She had a journal," Aunt Letty repeated.

"Where is it?"

Aunt Letty snickered. "Well, if I knew, I would've read it and given it to you by now. But I don't. Harriet was pretty clever, as I'm sure you recall."

Agatha nodded, silently taking note of a new mission: *find Aunt Hattie's journal.* As if she didn't have a hundred other things to do. "What's in the journal?"

Aunt Letty turned to look at Agatha. "Everything, I imagine. And I've looked everywhere."

Agatha got up and put her plate in the sink alongside her aunt's. "Did Aunt Hattie ever tell you about Blanche Caillavet?"

Aunt Letty quickly put a finger in front of Agatha's mouth, her finger smushing her top lip up toward her nose. "Shush! Right now. Do NOT say that name in this house." She looked around frantically as if the very mention of the name might've conjured the spirit of Blanche Caillavet into Aunt Hattie's home.

"I have your book," Agatha said, desperate to change the subject.

Aunt Letty raised her eyebrows in surprise. "Good."

"But I have some questions about it."

The eyebrows dropped. "Go on," she said, taking a seat at the table and folding her hands in front of her. Agatha saw her swallow. "But talk quietly." Aunt Letty peered around the corner at Tobie, who was lightly snoring, his legs in a weird pretzel-like arrangement on the couch. "I don't talk about these things in front of October," she said, using his full name.

"I'm on my second ghost," Agatha began.

Aunt Letty stared at her.

"Of five."

Aunt Letty continued to stare at her.

"My friend stole your book and used it to conjure her dead brother."

Aunt Letty sighed.

"And she invoked a Deceiver instead of her brother."

At this, Aunt Letty stood up, poured herself a glass of water and stood at the sink again, staring out the window into the backyard. "I knew it," she said.

Agatha continued. "The Deceiver tore out the pages of the epilogue. I need those pages, Aunt Letty, and I thought you might know what they said."

Aunt Letty took another sip of her water but said nothing.

Agatha fiddled with her thumbs but didn't put them in her mouth. "Do you know what the epilogue said?"

"No."

"So, you don't know what those pages said?"

"No." Aunt Letty was speaking in nearly a whisper, resigned to the reality of her answer. She hung her head, taking another sip of her water.

Agatha finally gave in, jamming one of the thumbs into her mouth. "I need to find the author, then. Is J. Wiltz local? The book looks homemade. I don't know what else to do."

Tobie stirred on the couch, rolling over and making a few low noises, trying to get comfortable in the cramped space. Aunt Letty waited until he was quiet again to continue. She took a couple of deep breaths, her ample chest rising and falling heavily. "I...I know J. Wiltz."

Agatha's eyes widened. "You do?"

Aunt Letty put her finger to her lips, looking over at Tobie again. "Bring the book to my bedroom."

Agatha jumped from the chair and scurried down the hallway, fishing the book out of her bag. She pushed open Aunt Letty's bedroom door and set the book on her nightstand, taking a seat on the small bed. Again, she glanced at the photograph of Aunt Hattie when she was a child, staring hard at it as if the girl in the picture would tell her where her missing journal was. *Maybe I can ask HattieCat,* she thought, storing that away in her memory's to do list.

Aunt Letty appeared in the doorway, a serious expression across her face. Her eyes hard and intense, her hair pulled in a tight little half bun at the top of her head, her black glasses magnifying her already intense brown eyes. She crossed the room and sat on the edge of the bed next to Agatha and took her hand.

"I know who J. Wiltz is, but she won't give you any answers."

"She?" said Agatha. Suddenly, the situation was becoming uncomfortable, but she dared not scoot away from Aunt Letty. Agatha looked back at the book as her aunt reached for it, stroking the cover of it, her fingers crossing the letters in the title. The expression on Aunt Letty's face changed from serious to despondent, the curves of her mouth arching downward and her lips beginning to tremble.

Agatha leaned toward her aunt. "Who is J. Wiltz, Aunt Letty?"

Aunt Letty exhaled the words, releasing information that unburdened her very soul. "J. Wiltz is Aunt Hattie."

CHAPTER 30
MIMICA!

"It's a pen name," Aunt Letty explained. "She wrote the book and then tried to hide it, hoping it would never see the light. She even made the cover herself." Her aunt ran her fingers over the binding and gave it a squeeze. "I found it at the shop and tried to keep it hidden. I had it on the desk the day your friend happened to come into the shop, and she took it." She looked at Agatha. "I was desperate to get it back, as you know."

"Yes."

"You see, Agatha, I know what the book can do. It was incredibly important I get the book back, but apparently, I was too late."

"Why did Aunt Hattie write it in the first place?"

"To summon our brother, I think."

At this, Agatha stood up, aghast. "Uncle Timmy?" she said aloud.

"Shhhhh." Aunt Letty patted the bed, motioning for her to sit. "Yes. You see, Harriet was concerned...." she paused. "Concerned the body, in the grave, you know, wasn't his."

Agatha was shocked. "What?"

Aunt Letty shook her head. "Yes, I know. But well, he did come home, just not his full self. Does that make sense?"

"Yes." Agatha distinctly remembered her father saying parts of Uncle Tim were fake in his casket, a result of the mine he'd stepped on in the war.

"Right," Aunt Letty continued. "Harriet wanted to make sure it *was* indeed our brother in that casket, so she tried to conjure him with a spell, but invoked a Deceiver instead. Ultimately, she wrote this book—and that epilogue you're desperately needing—from her experience. So, the same thing happened to your Aunt Hattie, but I'm not sure she ever got the answer she was looking for. About Uncle Tim, I mean." Aunt Letty was silent, resting her head in her hands. "Like I said, I have a feeling what she didn't share with me is in that journal."

Aunt Letty was quiet for a moment. "Regardless, you need that epilogue," she said, finally. "Yes," Agatha agreed.

"But I never read the epilogue. I haven't read any of the book. I was only protecting it." Aunt Letty gestured around the room. "Just like everything else. I've protected all of it. Every single thing Harriet has done has been with intention, and I don't want to disrupt that intention. Things are in their places for a reason. My sister always had a reason."

Agatha turned to face the numerous mirrors lining the walls, offering her aunt protection and solace. Insignificant material objects to others. A lifeline to Aunt Hattie.

"Have you..." Agatha paused, purposely avoiding saying his name. "...been to the Benford-O'Malley Funeral Home?"

"I know who you're talking about," said Aunt Letty without properly answering the question. She put the small book in her nightstand, closing the top drawer gently and slowly, as if to not disturb the power of the words written on its pages.

Agatha stood up, pacing the room, one of her knuckles between her front teeth. She went to put the other hand at her side and groaned. Still no pockets. She should've brought the jeans her mother bought her. Didn't they automatically come with pockets?

"I'm guessing you've been there," Aunt Letty said, her arms folded across her chest.

"Yes."

"Harriet did tell me once that he," Aunt Letty paused. "I don't want to say his name. But 'he' often spoke in riddles or in a way that was difficult to understand. As if he gave you the answer you sought, but you had to sift through his words to find it."

Agatha nodded. Nikolai's words were like mud, thick and heavy, but somewhere in the sludge might be a diamond.

"So, what did he tell you?"

Agatha shrugged. "I don't know. That Deceivers ultimately kill whatever it is they're copying. They're like—what was that word he used? Copies? No, that wasn't it." Agatha bit the side of her lip and snapped her fingers. "Mimics."

Aunt Letty nodded.

"Shapeshifters. That's what he said. A perfect replica."

Aunt Letty furrowed her brow. She retrieved the book from her nightstand and flipped through it vigorously, on a mission. "There has to be something in here." She opened the back part of the book and ran her fingers along the torn pages and slammed the book closed with a sigh. "Anything else?"

"He came to me in a dream. Before I went and saw him, I mean. I didn't get a chance to ask him about this, but he told me to 'find the light.'"

Aunt Letty was nibbling a thumb nail now, and Agatha tried to reign in her amusement.

"Light has many meanings, not just the ordinary one. I doubt 'he' meant sunlight or light as we know it."

Agatha took a seat again on the bed.

Aunt Letty's brow was still furrowed. "What was that word you used a moment ago?"

"Mimics?"

"No. Not replica either. The other—"

"Shapeshifters." A deep voice echoed in the hallway outside Aunt Letty's door. Tobie's brown eyes peered from around the doorframe, followed by the rest of him. In his arms, he carried his laptop. "I know a lot about those."

Agatha sighed. "You don't even believe in any of this stuff."

"Ah," Tobie said. "True." He opened the laptop and produced what looked like several thin, colorful paper magazines. Agatha immediately knew what they were. "However, I DO believe in a good comic book."

He handed them to Agatha. "In fact, this is my favorite. And she just so happens to be a shapeshifter."

Agatha and Aunt Letty stared at the cover, its large red letters with jagged ends emblazoned across the top in a scream: MIMICA!

Tobie continued. "I have every single edition involving Mimica, and I've collected them for years. Which means, I know an awful lot about shapeshifters. But most importantly, it means I can be of assistance with one very crucial detail."

Agatha looked up from the comic. “What’s that?”

Tobie’s eyes seared right through her. “I know what destroys a shapeshifter.”

CHAPTER 31
THE HEAD IN THE WATER

Tippy Trinkle decided she couldn't sleep or maybe was afraid to, though she didn't often like to admit to feeling fearful. She tiptoed down the circular stairs to the kitchen and poured herself a glass of milk, the light from the refrigerator casting shadows in the Trinkle family's large kitchen. She listened as she sipped, the quiet around her more unnerving than usual because she didn't feel alone.

Back in her room, she opened the two glass doors which led out to the second-floor balcony. The February air hit her thin pajamas with a punch, and she grabbed her favorite blanket, striped with every single color forming a rainbow. Her grandmother had made the blanket before she was born and died before she was six months old, so she couldn't possibly have known. Tippy smiled and wrapped it around herself, inhaling the scents of home.

Despite her long hair, makeup, and clothes, Tippy's outward appearance was not a mirror image to what she felt on the inside. Her exterior was at a constant war with her innards, which craved sports, admired fast cars, loved tools, fishing, camping, the gym, and all things of the earth. She loved to get her hands dirty, especially when her father let her use the weed eater or lawnmower, which wasn't often. The Trinkle family usually paid people to do those things.

Tippy sat in one of the wooden rocking chairs on the balcony and wrapped the blanket around her shoulders. She crossed her ankle on her knee—the unladylike way of sitting her mother often reminded her—and snickered. Who wanted to be a lady? She opened her phone to see if Agatha had responded to her last text, but she hadn't. A pang of disappointment settled in her belly.

Tippy's gaze fell upon the beach in the distance, the brown Biloxi water gently slurping the shore. Several cars passed, but midnight on a February Saturday morning was quiet. The moon wasn't full but was bright enough to cast a silver glow on the water beneath it. In the distance, Deer Island's trees darkened the horizon, their barren limbs crooked and awkward and silhouetted against the night sky. Like old peoples' hands, Tippy thought, with their knobby knuckles and fingers splayed in painful, arthritic directions.

A buoy bobbed in the black water, and low tide revealed several sandbars near the shore. Tippy kept her eyes on the buoy, which seemed to bounce roughly against the otherwise placid, dark water. She squinted, wondering what was causing the irregular movements when suddenly, a circular form appeared near its base. The form began to reveal more of itself, becoming larger until Tippy audibly whimpered.

The circle shape was a head.

She dropped her blanket and ran inside to her closet, fumbling with a few old shoes boxes before she found what she was looking for: an old pair of binoculars she and her brother used to use at night to spy on the neighbors. She hurried back to the balcony and placed the binoculars to her eyes with trembling hands.

The shape was larger now and moving. Tippy watched in horror as the head led to a neck and chest, followed by a torso, legs, and feet, all clothed in a long, gown that at one time used to be white. The figure reached the shore, dry and unaffected by the water. Every few steps, Tippy could make out several rotting toes which peeked beneath the gown and gripped the sand.

Tippy lowered the binoculars to her side, her eyes still on the woman who slowly crossed Beach Boulevard toward Tippy's home. The figure reached the edge of the Trinkle family's lawn and smiled up at Tippy before breaking into a run toward the front door.

CHAPTER 32
DEAR AGATHA

Leopold Panic tiptoed down the hallway to the third room in his small home which used to be his grandfather Dominicus' room. He tugged on the first drawer of an old wooden dresser and rummaged through a pile of papers and envelopes until he found the box he was looking for. An ornate crow embellished the cover of the box, its feathers made of black sequins with a beak painted gold and housed his mother's most expensive stationery.

He gently removed the top and pulled out three thick pieces of paper with one large black crow on each in the top left corner. The crow's eyes were hard and stern, as if keeping watch over the stationery itself.

Leopold pulled the door closed and paused in front of his mother's bedroom. In the darkness, he could see her form, lying on her side, her shoulders rising and falling with the gentle breath of sleep. He tucked a few small strands of hair behind his ear and laid his hand on the knob of her door, slowly pulling it closed.

Back in his room, Leopold put his backpack on his shoulders and looked around, figuring he wouldn't need much for this excursion. He sat at his desk with the stationery in front of him. The tip of his black pen rested against the ridged paper, creating a dot of ink as he collected his thoughts. He took a couple deep breaths and quickly scribbled.

Dear Agatha...

CHAPTER 33
THE GRIN OF A THOUSAND TEETH

Agatha smirked at Tobie. "Tell me."

"So," he began, taking a seat on the edge of his mother's bed next to Agatha. "I heard that whole conversation." He put his hands up. "I was NOT eavesdropping. I heard you guys talking, and I made the decision to listen."

Agatha wasn't buying it. "Mm-hmm."

"Yes, it was a conscious decision to listen and then reveal myself when necessary. I don't consider that eavesdropping. Eavesdropping is defined as 'secretly listening to a conversation.' See, it wasn't really 'in secret' because I had every intention of revealing myself. In fact—"

"Tobie," Aunt Letty interrupted him. "I'm going to get another cup of coffee." She laid a hand on her son's shoulder. "Get to the point."

Tobie nodded. "I heard you say that the creature in the funeral home appeared to you in a dream, right? Telling you to find the light or look for the light or something like that?"

Agatha nodded.

"See, the two things that can harm, incapacitate or destroy a shape-shifter are silver and fire."

Agatha stared at him. "Ok."

Both were silent as they decided who would speak next.

"Ok?" Agatha said finally. "But where's the light come in?"

Tobie rolled his eyes and stood up. "Dude, don't you have any good science teachers? Ok, lemme explain. Both of those two things—silver and fire—are almost synonymous with light, if you want to look at it that way. Fire obviously provides light. It *is* light." He paused, sarcasm spreading over his face in a ripple. "You do understand that part, right?"

"Shut up."

"Ok, ok. Silver, on the other hand, is a transition metal which exhibits the highest reflectivity of any metal. I mean, it has super high electrical conductivity and thermal conductivity capabilities as well, but that's for another conversation." He looked at Agatha who put her head in her hands.

"What?" she huffed through her fingers.

"Good grief, let me dumb it down for you. Silver is super reflective and responds directly to the intensity of a light source. In fact, the metallic shine of silver is because of a mirror-like reflection of light."

Agatha stared at him. "Tobie, please."

He sighed, grabbing the comics from her lap and speaking a babyish tone. "Silver is shiny. Verrrrrry shiny. It reflects light. Like, A LOT." He paused to laugh at himself. "Essentially, some people could attribute that or sort of say that silver is synonymous with light. Get it?"

"Ok, yes."

"Maybe that's what the creature was insinuating. Either silver or fire. Find the light, in a way, without coming out and directly saying so."

Agatha narrowed her eyes at Tobie. "How did you know he was a creature?"

Tobie's mouth fell open and for a moment, he did not have an answer. She'd stunned him.

Agatha smiled. All that intelligence, and now he was speechless. She pointed a finger at him. "Seriously. How did you know there was a creature in the funeral home, Tobie?"

Tobie stood up and went to the door. "Just a guess, I guess. I'm going to get some water."

Agatha stood too. "Tobie!" she demanded.

He stopped mid step in the doorway, his back to her for a few moments, deciding something. He turned to face her, his expression pained and filled with reluctance. Now it was Agatha's turn to be stunned. "Because I saw him," Tobie whispered, looking at his feet. "Isn't that what you want to hear? He was looking at me. The grin of a thousand teeth in that window."

CHAPTER 34
THE FLOATING WOMAN

The binoculars fell from Tippy's hand with a thud against the wood of the porch, and she grabbed her phone as she dashed to her room and down the spiral stairs. She stood on the last step and watched the front door, her dainty hand gripping the banister. For a few minutes, everything was quiet. She finally sat and opened her phone, her shaking fingers having trouble finding the letters to text Agatha.

She's here. I think! Help!

Her fingers slipped off the smooth face of her phone as she hit send. A movement at the front door caught her eye, and she abruptly stood up, her chest heaving with adrenaline. She stared as the wooden door turned white, followed by a flash of light, which blinded her.

She started to scramble up the stairs backwards, using her hands and feet to propel her upwards. Through her squinting eyes, she saw the figure again who, this time, was unmistakable.

An elderly woman, her yellowish grey hair atop her head in a bun, wearing a high-necked gown stood in Tippy Trinkle's house, staring at her. She smiled, and the darkness of death oozed from her lips, running down her chin slowly, sluggish in its thickness. She began to float toward Tippy, her toes dragging against the black and white tiles of the Trinkle family foyer.

Tippy tried to scream and scrambled on all fours toward her bedroom as the woman's hoarse voice croaked out a threat.

"I told you I wasn't going anywhere."

CHAPTER 35
THE TRADE

Leopold set his pen down, grabbed his backpack and opened his window, quietly jumping to the grass beneath. Both the front and back doors of the Panic house groaned when being opened, and he knew his mother was a light sleeper. Seeing a tire was flat on one of the bikes, Leopold stomped his foot on the concrete of the carport. The orange, rusty one would have to do, and he was thankful for it. He rode one street over to Agatha's house, which he found completely dark with no cars in the driveway.

Had they gone somewhere? *Good.* He'd no intention of speaking to Agatha, only leaving her a note, so this worked perfectly. He knew she'd try to stop him or her words would convince him to stop himself, and he didn't want either of those scenarios.

The white cat in the window stared at him from behind the glass as Leopold rounded the house toward the backyard. By the time he was at Agatha's bedroom window, the cat was too, again looking at him, its eyes glaring out some sort of warning.

HattieCat knows, he thought.

Leopold stared at the piece of stationery, folded neatly into what was meant to be the shape of a swan, an origami trick his mother had taught him years ago. He'd tried for a crow but failed miserably, and this looked more like a chicken with large wings and an exaggerated beak. It would have to do. The wood of Agatha's window frame was splintered and cracked, the paint peeling in all directions, and he wedged the paper bird's beak in between it. He hoped Agatha would see it sooner rather than later.

He grabbed his bike in the driveway, momentarily pausing to meet eyes again with HattieCat, who'd resumed her post at the front window. He took a quick trip through the cemetery, and looked back at Agatha's house, his note still stuck tightly in the window frame. Leopold's stare drifted from Agatha's house upward toward the navy sky and the moon, a sentry patrolling the night, its light guiding Leopold Panic's path toward his destination and the darkness which lay beyond it.

***

He laid his bike in the grass behind the Benford-O'Malley Funeral Home and looked at the window he'd crawled through twice, though this time was different. Leopold had never been alone.

He stole a quick glance around to make sure the midnight hour offered him enough coverage as he pried open the window and slithered through. Once inside, he sat beneath it and rummaged through his backpack, his hands not finding what they wanted. He'd forgotten his flashlight.

Leopold punched the bag. How could he be so stupid? But did it matter? He couldn't see Lucius Nikolai anyway.

Leopold kept his shoes on as he tiptoed down the long hallway, pausing every few steps to look at each of the former funeral director's photographs adorning the wall. Each bore the last name Benford or O'Malley, and none were Lucius Nikolai. The waiting room's fireplace sat dark and quiet as Leopold positioned himself against a wall facing the room and sat on the floor. He looked around, and after a few moments, cleared his throat.

"Mr. Nikolai?" he said aloud, but it came out in more of a whisper. The silence gave him the impression of being alone, but Leopold knew that to be a lie.

Suddenly, the composition of the air shifted. There was a tangible heaviness, the temperature dropped, and Leopold shivered. He felt the powerful urge to sit in one of the chairs beside the fireplace and did so, his movements slow and methodical as if in a trance. A pressure started around his wrists and worked its way up both arms until two weights like hands rested on his shoulders, and Leopold knew who was behind him.

Lucius Nikolai rounded the chair and leaned into Leopold's face, though the boy couldn't see or hear him. "Good of you to come, Mr. Panic. You know, I was really hoping it would've been Agatha Anxious who touched the Deceiver." He extended his hand, a long brown fingernail nearly touching Leopold's chin. "But you'll do just fine."

CHAPTER 36
SHAPESHIFTERS FOR DUMMIES

Agatha swallowed. "How did you see him?"

Tobie ran a hand through his hair. "Can we please not discuss that? I don't know. I really don't, and I honestly don't even care to find out. The one thing I DO know is I won't be driving you to Benford-O'Malley again, ok? So don't even ask."

"Are you a Perceiver?" She heard her phone chirp in her bedroom, but she ignored it.

"What?" Tobie shouted, then lowered his voice. "What is that, even? A ghost seer? No! And I don't want to be one either. Stop it."

Agatha bit her lip. Tobie might be done with that conversation, but she wasn't. She would, however, put it on hold.

"Back to the shapeshifter..." he demanded.

"Ok," she nodded, reluctantly. "Back to the shapeshifter. Silver or fire?"

"Yes."

Agatha had a brief thought, which dissipated when reality hit her. Aunt Hattie's silver spiral necklace.

"What?"

"Hmm?"

"What did you just think? Right then. I saw your face." Tobie asked.

"Aunt Hattie had a silver spiral necklace. It was important to her."

"Well, where is it?"

Agatha's mind wandered to the white fluffy cat which was undoubtedly snoozing on her bed at the moment, a black spiral design on its chest. "It's uh, missing. Like her. She never took it off, so it's wherever she is."

"Too bad. That might've helped."

"That leaves fire. There's no way for me to bring fire to the old hospital, somehow throw it on the Deceiver—who's awfully quick, by the way—and somehow what, burn it to death? It's already dead, right?"

Tobie shook his head. "Is THAT what you were doing in the hospital? I don't even want to know. Forget it."

Agatha shook her head. "No. This seems too complicated, Tobie. It has to be simpler than this."

"It's not really that complicated, as I see it. What's difficult? Fire or silver. That's your answer. That's your 'light.'"

"No. I can't help this gut feeling that it's something simpler than that. Aunt Hattie always told me to go with my gut."

"Well, I can't argue with that. Intuition is a powerful thing."

Agatha sighed, exhausted. "Maybe silver. Maybe I'll focus on that. I don't know." She motioned to Tobie to give her one of the comic books. The inside pages revealed a buxom female with a small waist, muscular arms and legs, black knee-high boots, and purple hair. Her eyes were white, and she was clothed in a black bikini. She looked up at Tobie. "Yeah, I see why you like Mimica."

"Give me more credit than that, Agatha." He snatched the comic away from her. He put them in order according to number. "Ok, so do you know much about shapeshifters? Maybe you should start there."

"More than I'd like to, but still not enough," Agatha responded, pushing a few stray pieces of bangs out of her eyes.

Tobie pointed to the comic books. "Mimica is the most powerful shapeshifter. She was created on planet—"

"Can you just kinda give me the highlights? You know, the major points."

"Well, that's not really a quick conversation. I mean, shapeshifters are complicated, intricate creatures."

"Tobie."

"Ok, ok. Shapeshifters for dummies. Gotcha."

"Uggggghhhhhh," Agatha groaned, heading to her bedroom. Tobie followed.

"Ok, fine. They're super powerful creatures that can mimic absolutely anything."

"Do you know how silly you sound?" She heard her phone chirp again.

"Me?" Tobie's voice hinted at irritation. "I sound silly?"

"Yeah. You don't believe in ghosts, but you believe in this stuff?"

Tobie tightened his grip on his beloved comics. "I didn't say I believed in it. But I am saying I know a lot about shapeshifters. And you don't."

"You're a dork," Agatha smiled, trying to smooth over the situation.

"No, you are," Tobie smirked too.

"Continue with your dorkiness."

"Ok," Tobie said, ignoring her. "They can replicate even the tiniest details of a person or object. Big things and small things. Mannerisms, powers, abilities, how they speak, among other things. Clothing too, of course. Features. Accents. Gait. Things like that."

Agatha stopped. "Powers?"

"Of course. You name it."

"Powers?" she repeated.

"Uh, yeah?"

Tippy's last words to Agatha rang in her ears. *I think I saw a woman. A woman in white.* "A woman in white," she said aloud to herself.

"Who?"

"The Deceiver. It can be Big or Blanche or whomever it wants to be..."

"Who?" Tobie repeated, sounding like an owl.

"Which means also the Deceiver can have all of the abilities and power and memories and anger of Blanche Caillavet..."

"Wait, what?" Tobie changed his wording.

Agatha grabbed him, her small grip pinching the skin of his forearm. "Tippy!" Agatha ran to her bedroom and snatched her phone off the bed. "Oh no," she said as she read the missed text from Tippy.

She's here. I think! Help!

Agatha looked at Tobie. "We have to go! Now!"

CHAPTER 37
THE CLOSET

Tippy crawled past her brother's bedroom, into her own and lunged for her closet, which did not lock from the inside. She buried herself between her clothes, her breaths coming out in exaggerated puffs which made it harder to breathe in the small space. She tried to open her prior text to Agatha, unsure whether it had sent.

The handle to her closet door began to turn, and Tippy Trinkle let out a small cry. The darkness camouflaged her as several grey fingers gripped the inside of the door frame. A foul odor filled the small closet like a fog, and Tippy took one long breath and held it.

The Woman in White had come for her.

CHAPTER 38
THE REAL ANSWER

In some ways, Aunt Letty was just like Aunt Hattie. She didn't ask any questions when Tobie suddenly informed her that he needed to run Agatha home. She gave him a quick hug and let them be on their way. Once in the cab of the truck, Agatha nibbled a middle finger—her least favorite finger to nibble—and wondered what her aunt truly thought.

Tobie barely stayed under the speed limit as they whizzed down Beach Boulevard toward Tippy's house. Agatha tried to text Leopold.

Are you up? She waited a few eternal moments, but he didn't answer. She figured he would've stayed up on a weekend night, but maybe not. She texted again.

*I'm heading to Tippy's house. I think the...*she paused, not wanting to say it in case his mother periodically checked his phone. She erased and started over. *I'm heading to Tippy's. I hope she's not in trouble. I'll let you know.*

"So, fire or silver? Whatcha gonna go with?" Tobie asked, clearly unaffected by the tenseness of the moment.

"I think we should talk about how you saw Lucius Nikolai," Agatha said bluntly. "I want to know."

"Well, I don't," Tobie shot back.

"You're not even slightly curious?"

"Not in the least. In fact, I'd rather forget it, if you can take a hint."

"Are y'all related?"

Tobie pressed the breaks in the middle of Beach Boulevard and pulled over to the side by the boardwalk. "What?"

"Aunt Hattie told me that ghosts appear to people in two ways. Well, I'm sure there's more than two ways. Maybe there isn't, but it seems like there would be—"

"Agatha," he interrupted her. "Get to the point."

She nodded. "You're either a Perceiver or related to Nikolai."

"No. No ma'am, I am NOT related to that, whatever he is."

"Well, I wouldn't think you are either."

"He's not even human. How could I be related to him?"

"Actually, he was human. He is the original owner and undertaker of the Benford-O'Malley Funeral Home. He just still.... lives...there."

"Wait a second. How is it called Benford-O'Malley if he were the original owner?" Tobie slowly pulled back out onto the road, looking both directions though they were the only car at that hour.

Agatha stared at the dark water of the gulf just outside her window. "Huh?"

"I mean if he's the owner wouldn't it be called the Nikolai Funeral Home or something? Even if it's passed hands and been handed down to different people in the family, like why isn't it named after him? It's named after two completely different people, ya know? Benford and O'Malley. I'm assuming that's two people, I mean."

Agatha furrowed her brow. "I...I don't know."

"What exactly do you go there for?"

"Why do I see him?"

"Yeah," Tobie said. "I don't really want the answer, but I'm having an idea."

"He's like, an oracle. He knows everything. Aunt Hattie told me he can help Perceivers. Perceivers are people who can see and help ghosts, by the way."

Tobie snorted. "An oracle. Ok. And *does* he help you?"

Agatha paused, unsure how to answer the question. "Kind of."

Tobie arched an eyebrow. "Kind of?"

"Yeah, he's shifty. He's a bit shady, I mean."

"Mmm." Tobie stared straight ahead as he sorted through a few thoughts. "Have you ever thought to look into Mr. Nikolai? Like, some historical research at the library or anything. You know, it might not all be chasing ghosts and intuition. Sometimes good old fashioned detective work means books, Agatha."

"No, I...no I haven't," she said. *Tobie might be onto something,* she thought.

"New assignment. Forget all this ghost and Deceiver stuff. I think you—"

"Very funny. I CAN'T just forget all this ghost and Deceiver stuff. These things are real and won't go away unless I do something about them." She flipped open her phone again. Still no response from Leopold.

Tobie rolled his eyes. "Real to you. Regardless, maybe you need to shift your focus."

"What's that mean?"

"Meaning, maybe the real answer lies with Lucius Nikolai."

CHAPTER 39
SUDDENLY, NOTHING AT ALL

The woman's face peeked through the crack of the door, and she gave Tippy a syrupy, dripping smile as a yellowy black ooze dripped from the corners of her mouth. Both hands gripped the closet doorframe tightly, her sinewy, thin grey arms bent in awkward directions like a spider. Several of her yellow fingernails cracked under her grip as she uttered a guttural giggle that sounded very much like a man.

Yet, just as the woman began to enter into the closet, her eyes became wild with surprise. She let go of the doorframe and hung, suspended in the air, her frail body starting to shake. She opened her mouth as her body stiffened, her fingers now warped in distorted, unsteady fists at her side. "No!" she started to say as her toes and feet crumbled into dust, the transformation working its way up her legs to her knees and thighs, then her stomach and torso and her chest. Her neck twisted and crumbled too, until nothing was left of her but her awful head. "NO!" Her husky, angry scream filled the space of Tippy's closet as the woman's face crinkled and wrinkled like a raisin before disappearing into dust.

Abruptly, everything stopped.

Tippy's eyes were clamped shut, her breath frozen in her lungs. When she could hold it no longer, she exhaled in a gasp, sputtering and coughing into one of her dresses that she held against her mouth. She opened one eye and saw that she was alone, her closet door completely shut as if nothing had happened. No decaying fingers gripping the doorframe. No stench in the closet. No floating head or oozing mouth. No woman whatsoever.

Tippy Trinkle was afraid to move. She waited another few minutes before opening her phone, her hands still trembling from the experience a few moments before. No response yet from Agatha.

"Stupid thing," she whispered to herself as she got to her knees but kept her eyes on the doorknob. It didn't turn. When she pressed an ear against the door, she detected no movement on the other side. It would be just like the Henry or the woman to be waiting to devour her, tricking her into thinking all was calm and safe. Tippy sat back down and scooted herself into a corner. Should she stay? Should she check?

She uttered a small, hoarse cry. "Mom?" There was no way her mother would hear that. She said it again, louder. "Mom!" Still nothing. Her parents' bedroom was downstairs. Of course, they wouldn't hear her from her closet. Why did she back herself into her own closet anyway? What a dumb move.

Tippy grabbed a wire coat hanger and untwisted it until the ends were like dull spikes. It was the only weapon she could find. Her sweaty palm reached for the doorknob and turned. She backed away again, waiting and listening. Nothing. She nudged the door open with her big toe and was met with the darkness and stillness of her bedroom. She had a clear view under her bed and her curtains were drawn open. The bedroom was empty.

“What in the world?” she whispered to herself. Something had just happened, something surprising and unexpected and unplanned to the woman. Something she wasn’t happy with. Tippy surveyed the landscape of her bedroom. Everything felt different. The air, the room, her own little body, like the weight of worry and fear and concern had completely and suddenly disappeared.

“Henry?” she said aloud. Silence.

Tippy went to her nightstand and flipped open her journal to the page where her brother had written her the note a few days ago. She stared hard at the pages, clean and white and pristine.

And blank.

CHAPTER 40
CRUMBLED

Tobie slowed as some of the large homes came into view on Biloxi Beach. "Is this it?" he said, pointing to one of the long driveways.

Agatha nodded. "Yeah, pull in and turn off the truck."

He did as he was told while Agatha texted Tippy.

I'm here. Are your parents home? I don't want to knock. Is everything ok??

Agatha waited while her mind still juggled Tobie's thoughts about Lucius Nikolai. It hadn't occurred to her that Nikolai was possibly the problem and not the solution simply because Aunt Hattie had steered her in his direction. Well, sort of. And Aunt Hattie's words were always of divine meaning, those to be followed, believed, and never questioned. Right?

Tippy suddenly appeared on the balcony of her home, her silk pajamas wrinkled, the top hanging off one of her shoulders. Agatha squinted to make sure that was her before exiting the truck. She ran to the edge of the porch, calling up to Tippy.

"Where is she?"

Tippy shook her head, her black hair falling in wispy strands from her ponytail. "I, I don't know. Everything just stopped."

"Stopped?"

"Yeah, like, she disappeared right as she was about to get me!" Agatha could see Tippy's bottom lip tremble from where she stood.

"Are you ok?"

Tippy exhaled. "Someday I will be. Not tonight, but someday. I think it's over Agatha," she squatted and peered at Agatha from between the wooden railing. She looked like a child, Agatha thought, small and timid and afraid. Uncertainty and bewilderment flooded Tippy from head to toe.

"It's over? But where did she go?"

"I don't know. She screamed 'no!' and then like, sort of crumbled." Tippy sniffled and wiped her nose with her sleeve. "And that was it."

"Crumbled?" Agatha said.

"And then everything changed. Like, I *feel* different, Agatha. I don't know how to describe it." Tippy's voice became softer as she sniffled again. "Like everything might actually be...ok."

Agatha stood on Tippy's lawn, confused and wondering if she should leave. There didn't seem to be any danger any longer, which she couldn't reconcile with Tippy's text thirty minutes ago. Tippy might feel better, but Agatha felt worse, like something else had happened that she couldn't put her finger on.

"Ok," she finally said. "Um...call me if she comes back, ok? Like, immediately."

Tippy nodded, straightening her pajama top on her shoulders. She picked up her rainbow blanket by the rocking chair and slid her glass door closed without saying goodbye.

CHAPTER 41
RIDDLES

Tobie drove Agatha home, every so often stealing a glance in her direction. Agatha could tell he wanted to ask questions but didn't. That would be showing too much interest in things he supposedly didn't believe in. Once at the Anxious house, Tobie lingered in his doorway, staring at Agatha as she made her way down the hallway to her bedroom. She heard him call Aunt Letty as she face-planted into her comforter.

"Mom? We're here. Yeah. Mm-hmm. Ok. Love you too."

The clock next to her bed read 2:02 am, and Agatha knew sleep wouldn't come, even though her body felt tired. Her mind was wide awake, twelve different scenarios, problems, solutions, and new scenarios leading to more problems bouncing around her brain as if it were a spongy trampoline. She texted Leopold again, knowing he was probably asleep.

Everything is ok but weird. It shouldn't be ok on its own because I didn't do anything. I don't get it. Talk tomorrow?

She ended her text with a question. It wasn't like Leopold to not respond to her, no matter the hour. She stuck a pinkie into the corner of her mouth, but didn't bite down, using one of her canine teeth to gently rub against the nail while she was deep in thought.

"Hey."

Agatha sat up in her bed, startled.

Tobie handed her a warm mug. "Doesn't look like you're going to bed anytime soon."

"Hot chocolate? Why are you being nice?"

"Who, me? I'm not nice," he headed back toward his bedroom.

Agatha grabbed her backpack, shuffling through until she found the folder she was looking for. She opened it, the Black History Month quotes staring back at her for the hundredth time. She started to reread them, but her eyes froze on the first one.

Darkness cannot drive out darkness; only light can do that.
Hate cannot drive out hate; only love can do that.

– Martin Luther King, Jr.

She read and reread it repeatedly, until her eyes were dry, and her heart did cartwheels inside her chest. Only light could drive out darkness. What a coincidence. Is that what Lucius meant by finding the light? It had to be. Light was the only way to get rid of darkness. Another thing that had been in front of her the whole time. Why couldn't

Lucius just say so? Why did he have to speak in twisted phrases meant to confuse, puzzle, and perplex?

Lucius Nikolai. Who was he, really?

Agatha hopped off her bed and ran to Tobie's bedroom. "Hey, can I use your laptop for a minute?"

"For what?"

"For precisely what you told me to do."

She waited for the laptop to boot up and promptly opened Google, typing in Benford-O'Malley Funeral Home. She clicked on the "About Us" tab and then "Our History." She skimmed through several of the staff's biographies and some of the older pictures of the Benford-O'Malley Funeral Home, but there was nothing mentioning Lucius Nikolai. A small paragraph noted the funeral home had been acquired by the O'Malley Family in the 1960s but did not specify from whom or why.

Agatha stared at Tobie. "Guess what?"

Tobie wound a piece of floss around his fingers and proceeded to clean between his teeth. "Hmm?"

"Nothing on the Benford-O'Malley website about Lucius Nikolai."

Tobie shook his head, his tongue working a space between his bottom front teeth. "Told you. Google him specifically," he said as Agatha's fingers punched the keys.

Her eyes landed on the first image that popped up, a black and white portrait of a tall, thin man with slicked back jet-black hair and a pencil thin mustache. He wore a three-piece suit, his hands tucked in his pockets, and he stood outside a business with columns that Agatha immediately recognized. The Benford-O'Malley Funeral Home.

She squinted to make out the man's features, though she already knew it to be Lucius Nikolai. His angular face. Pointed bird's beak of a nose and dark eyes. No grey skin, two sets of eyelids or pointed teeth, though. What had done that? Death? To his right was the business's original sign, which read "Eternal Light Funeral Home. Undertaker, Lucius Nikolai."

Several pictures showed him in and around the funeral home. One pictured him behind the large desk in the meeting room. Another featured him sitting in his chair by the fireplace, and Agatha felt a chill wiggle its way up her spine. *His favorite chair.* A final picture showed him shaking hands with another gentleman who wasn't smiling. Perhaps a mourner.

She scrolled the pages, finding nothing else. Nothing about what had happened to the Eternal Light Funeral Home or Lucius Nikolai himself. But it wasn't the absence of articles that startled Agatha. Instead, it was the presence of other articles that popped up, seemingly unrelated, when she searched Nikolai's name.

There, beneath two pictures of Lucius Nikolai were several articles about the arrest of a local woman who'd once been a suspect in the disappearance of a local boy named Bobby Calvert. The boy had last been seen at her shop in Vieux Marche, and a Biloxi policeman had found his wristwatch there.

In the article, the woman glared at the camera from the backseat of a police car, her arms behind her presumably in handcuffs, her red lips pursed together in determination. Agatha knew the face no matter the time nor place nor circumstance. She'd see it in her dreams, in her waking moments, and in her nightmares. She'd seen this woman young, old, and in death's stages of decay. And Agatha would know that face until the very last breath of her life filled every curvature, corner, and alcove of her lungs.

Slowly, her eyes fell to the italicized caption beneath the picture, though she knew she didn't need to read it.

Blanche N. Caillavet, former Mardi Gras Queen of Biloxi and owner of Blanche's Baubles & Beads, is arrested Thursday on suspicion of kidnapping.

Tobie heard Agatha gasp from the bathroom where he was now washing his face. "What? What is it?" he yelled, appearing in the doorway with water dripping off his chin.

Agatha was on her feet, pacing the hallway now. "Two things." She looked at Tobie whose expectant expression urged her to continue. It was a long story, and Tobie had no idea who Blanche even was, not to mention Agatha's encounters with her. "Um, nevermind. Ghost stuff."

His face fell. "Oh."

She had to talk to someone who would understand, though, and she opened her phone. It was nearly 3:00 am now, and certainly Leopold wouldn't respond this time either, but it was important for him to know this information when he woke up.

I did some research on Nikolai. Two things. 1) Blanche owned a shop in Vieux Marche. Sounds like a bead or Mardi Gras shop. Do you think that's where Doom's Maskerades is now? I mean she was haunting that back room, ya know? 2) When I searched Lucius Nikolai, stuff about Blanche came up. Why? 3) (Did I say there would be two things? There's three) Blanche was arrested years ago for the disappearance of a boy. Bobby something.

Agatha paused, her eyes darting back and forth in her skull as the hint of a memory passed before them. Leopold doing a jig and dancing while he recited that little poem about Blanche in the cemetery that day. What was it? Something about not waiting too late to visit Blanche Caillavet's shop.

"Ughhhhhh," she groaned, throwing herself back on her bed, trying earnestly to remember Leopold's words. Something about her asking riddles too. He'd said it was a local saying. Who else would know? Aunt Hattie surely would, and maybe Aunt Letty would, though Aunt Letty didn't like discussing such things.

Too bad.

Agatha dialed Aunt Letty's number. She was going to ask anyway. Aunt Letty picked up on the third ring. "Yes?" she said, her voice foggy with sleep.

"Aunt Letty, I'm sorry. I have to ask something that is going to make you mad."

"What?"

Agatha didn't repeat herself. "Blanche Caillavet—"

"Agatha!" Aunt Letty's tone was serious.

"I said I was sorry," Agatha said, continuing despite her aunt's protests. "There's a little poem or saying about her that locals know. About riddles and her shop and don't go there when its dark or late or something. What is it?"

The other end of the phone was silent for a moment, but Agatha could hear Aunt Letty's breathing. Specifically, an irritated sigh. "Agatha," Aunt Letty started to say and then changed her mind, lowering her voice to a whisper. "Don't wait until the sun doth set to visit the shop of Blanche Caillavet. A riddle she'll ask to sell you a mask. You and your soul are the debt."

"That's it! Thank you—" Agatha said, scribbling quickly on a scrap of paper as Aunt Letty hung up in her face.

CHAPTER 42
THE IMPORTANCE OF LEOPOLD PANIC

Agatha woke, her fingers still wrapped around the piece of paper she'd written on a few hours before. Her mouth was sticky and dry, and she rubbed the crumbly remnants of sleep from the corners of her eyes. She looked to see if Leopold had responded. Nothing. *Where is he?* she thought, the beginnings of uncertainty weaseling their way inside her.

She headed for the front door, no need to get dressed as she'd fallen asleep in her clothes from yesterday. Her parents' car was parked in the driveway. They must've returned while she was asleep.

"Mom?" she called out.

"Mmm?" Her mother said from the kitchen.

"I'm going to walk over to Leopold's."

"What?"

"I'm going to walk over to Leopold's house. He lives one street over, remember?"

"Is Penny home?"

"I don't know," Agatha answered quickly, before she realized why her mother was asking. "Mom, really? I'm not even going into his house. I'll stand outside and talk. Is that ok?" Agatha rolled her eyes and yanked at the front door several times before it opened, the rotten wood at the bottom catching on the door frame.

"Ok," Anita Anxious said hesitantly. "I guess. But don't stay long. It's supposed to storm around five o'clock."

"But it's only—" she stopped as she read the wall clock in the living room. It was ten after four. She'd slept that long?

She nodded and stepped out into the pre-evening March air; February having expired just the day before. Her small boots clicked against the pavement as she left Azalea Drive for Gill Avenue. She recited the poem about Blanche Caillavet to herself as she walked, not wanting to forget it. She was sure there was a clue in there, maybe for use at a later time.

"Don't wait until the sun doth set," she said as she neared the end of her street and entered the vacant lot across from Leopold's house. "To visit the shop of Blanche Caillavet."

Her boots trudged through the weeds and overgrown grass, and a few droplets from the sky fell fat and heavy on her blonde hair. "A riddle she'll ask to sell you a mask." Some twigs cracked and crackled beneath her weight, and she kicked at a lone ant pile, its thousands of residents skittering every which way, awake and angry. "You and your soul are the debt."

She kicked at the ant pile once more as Leopold's peach colored house came into view, along with two police cars parked out front. She stopped and squatted behind a tree.

His mother, Penny, stood outside talking to an officer, a small spiral bound pad of paper in his hands. He was writing as she talked. Penny Panic's face was bright red and puffy, her watery eyes wide with worry. Agatha saw Leopold's window was slightly open, the parted curtains allowing full view into his empty room. She squinted to see further and suddenly felt Penny's gaze upon her.

"Agatha!" she called from across the street, motioning her over with the hand holding a wadded tissue.

Agatha reluctantly joined her by the police officer who introduced himself as Officer Moody. Penny sniffled as she tried to talk.

"I.... I woke up this morning, and Leopold was gone." A cry of pain caught in her throat, and she had to pause to keep her composure. "He left this." She handed Agatha a piece of paper folded into the shape of a frog. She opened her hand as Penny Panic placed the paper in her waiting palm.

"I can't believe he'd run away," she started to cry, covering her eyes with the already wet tissue.

Officer Moody addressed Agatha, attempting to be friendly despite the circumstances. "What is your name, miss?"

"Agatha," she said, gently unfolding the paper. "Agatha Anxious."

"And are you a friend of Leopold Panic?"

"Yes sir," she said, pausing, waiting to read the words Leopold had scribbled on the paper. It felt intrusive, words he'd meant for his mother, not Agatha. Why did Ms. Panic want her to read it?

"And do you have any idea where he might have gone, Agatha? If he were to have run away, I mean."

Agatha unfolded the paper, revealing a black crow in the corner.

Mom,

I will be back.

I don't know when but do not worry about me.

She handed the note back to Leopold's mother, whose fingers were shaking so badly she could hardly grasp it. Agatha wanted to tell Officer Moody there was no way Leopold would've run away. Too many things were happening. The Deceiver was still an issue. Wasn't it, or not? Lucius Nikolai still said things Agatha needed to figure out. Leopold needed to get his powers back. Wait, is that why he'd left? No. Leopold Panic would never leave Agatha Anxious. They were a team, weren't they?

Agatha felt a lump of great proportions form in the back of her throat. It wasn't mucus or spit or something that could be easily swallowed away. Instead, it was made of grief and concern and worry, the type of mournful gloom that is also felt in your heart and bounces off your soul, its sharp little edges wounding you every time you think about it. The kind of sorrow that's felt when you realize someone's importance only after they're gone. When it's too late.

Agatha had an inkling of what might have happened to Leopold, but she looked at Officer Moody with the beginnings of tears in her eyes and responded with the only thing that would make sense to adults who had no idea what was going on in the Perceiver world.

"I'm sorry, sir. I don't know," she said.

CHAPTER 43
BIG

Agatha flipped Officer Moody's business card between her fingers as she walked back home in a daze. She decided to skip going inside and opted to sit in her backyard instead. The sky mulled over whether or not to rain, every now and then releasing a few droplets and then changing its mind.

Anita Anxious poked her head out the back door. "Agatha."

Agatha heard her but didn't turn to face her. "Yes?"

"Um...Penny just called me."

Agatha didn't respond.

Her mother lingered in the doorway. "Let me know if you need anything, ok? I'm, I'm sure Leopold will be back," she said, unconvincingly.

Agatha shook her head so her mother could see it but still said nothing. She was unconvinced herself, especially if he'd gone to see Lucius Nikolai. Who knows what would have happened behind the walls of the Benford-O'Malley Funeral Home without a witness. Without Agatha.

Nighttime fell on Agatha Anxious as she sat, stoic, facing the cemetery. It comforted her, settling on her shoulders like a blanket, and she sighed. Every now and then she could hear the back door creak open, her mother probably peering out at her, wondering when she would come in. But Agatha had no intention of going back inside. She scowled into the night, her glare falling on several crooked headstones off in the distance, their rotting, silk flowers littering the grass. Her eyes remained fixed on the graves as she ran through the events of the last twenty-four hours over and over in her head, playing them in order from memory like scenes from a movie.

Coming home from school, heading to Aunt Letty's, the tacos, the chat with her aunt at the table, Tobie's comic books, the realization the Deceiver was most likely a copy of Blanche Caillavet, Tippy's text, she and Tobie rushing to Tippy's only to find everything was suddenly and surprisingly fine. Perfectly still and back to normal with no explanation. And during all of this, no response from Leopold.

A movement snapped her back to the present, and Agatha blinked a few times. Next to one of the old headstones was a pair of feet, and Big now sat cross-legged on one of the graves. He beckoned her to him with a small hand.

Agatha left her backyard, climbing over the chain-link fence, but she kept her eyes on him. Was this the Deceiver? He smelled earthy, a little bit like dirt, and his hands and feet were clean. He leaned against the headstone, toying with a stick in the dirt, drawing different lines and shapes, and Agatha was certain it was Big.

He looked at her as she took a seat in the grass a few feet away from him, being careful to sit off to the side of the grave and not on anyone's 'body.'

"Hi," he said, so low and soft Agatha wasn't sure whether the sound came from him or was a rush of the night wind. He smiled at her, exposing the gap between his front teeth. She was stunned.

"You...can talk?"

He nodded his head, his orange curls bouncing happily atop his head like gelatin in a bowl, and he smiled again. Agatha's face fell, and Big stopped smiling. If he could now talk, then she knew something had happened, just like the Deer Island Ghost didn't speak until he got his coin back.

"The Deceiver.... It's gone, isn't it?"

Big nodded again.

"How?"

He shrugged as he continued to play in the dirt.

"Do you not want to talk about it?"

Big jammed the stick into the ground, twirling out several letters. Agatha watched as his stick spelled out two words.

I can't.

She looked up at him and for a few moments they eyed one another, deciding who would say what next. Big looked around as if expecting someone.

"I'm dead, aren't I," he said, suddenly.

Agatha didn't know how to reply. She nodded.

He brushed the dirt off his hands. "I didn't know when I first visited you."

"Yes," she responded. "But I didn't either."

Big giggled. "I just showed up and you let me in, and we became friends. Just like that."

Agatha tried to match his happiness, but it felt wrong. "I know. It's ridiculous," she managed.

"We had fun at that hospital," he said, a smile puffing his cheeks. "Pushing all those buttons in the elevator and stuff that day."

"I was there? With you? Why?" Agatha asked.

"Your mom's friend...Mr. Carr, I think? He was sick." The smile slipped from his face, and he became serious. "That's why *you* were there, I mean. But I died there, didn't I?"

The memory dawned again on Agatha like the morning sun on the coast's horizon. It was one of the times Mr. Carr had been in the hospital, and she and her mother had visited him. And Big was there not because he'd accompanied Agatha but because he'd always been there. Since the day he passed away, his little ghost had walked and wandered those hallways. For a brief period of time he'd been lost, completely unaware he was dead. And that was when he met Agatha and followed her home. Indeed, the first time they met was at the Back Bay Hospital.

"Yes," Agatha finally answered.

"I thought so." Big sighed.

Suddenly, he stood. "Walk with me, Agatha," he whispered her name in an English accent, reminiscent of their days together long ago when he thought he was alive, and she did too. A sadness nestled itself into her belly as he led her to his grave at the front of the cemetery.

He hopped on top of his own headstone, his bare feet touching the marble which bore the name Henry Trinkle. "I only have a few more minutes," he said. The boy in front of her was quite different than the boy who'd once been her imaginary friend. He would eternally be a child but had somehow aged and matured in a way Agatha couldn't quite understand. Where had he been all this time? To learn things, to mature, to grow older, to *seem* older. Is that what Death did? She wanted to ask, but time was limited, and Big outstretched his palm, revealing something that was much more important than Agatha's questions: *the second shard of mirror glass.*

"For you," he smiled, as a curl fell in front of one of his eyes.

He laid it in her hand, and she curled her fingers around it, protectively. She frowned. "I don't deserve this."

Big looked at her.

"I didn't even do anything for this. I think someone else did."

"Oh, and this." He reached into the pocket of his tuxedo pants and produced a small, rolled-up piece of paper. He leaned forward as he handed it to her, whispering again in an English accent, "You don't know it yet, but this is more important than the glass."

His fingers lingered on the piece of paper, and he stared at Agatha, a wistful look sprinkled over his face. "Goodbye Agatha Anxious," he said, revealing his gap-toothed grin a final time and was gone.

Agatha stood on Henry Trinkle's grave in silence, taking in the night sounds around her. The traffic from Beach Boulevard drowned out the sounds of the waves on the beach, but she knew they were there. The waves and water forever lapping the shores of the Gulf Coast. Just because you couldn't hear or see something didn't mean it wasn't there. Like Aunt Hattie. Agatha knew she was with her even though she couldn't see her. Forever. She looked at the grass beneath her boots. Just like she knew Big's body was six feet beneath her. Forever, he would be there, too. And finally resting.

She walked back to her house and noticed the light in living room was still on. She said goodnight to her mother who smiled at her from the couch. Agatha made her way to her bedroom where she shut the door and clicked on the lamp by her bed. She stared at the piece of glass and paper in her hand, reluctant to open the message knowing it was the last communication she'd ever receive from Big.

She hadn't missed him until recently. Not at all, really, but seeing him again had stirred feelings of nostalgia and longing she didn't know she had. Weird feelings deep within her, and now that they'd surfaced, she almost wished they'd disappear. Big represented a piece of her childhood. One that presented itself as fun and sweet and innocent but perhaps had been none of those. Knowing he was a real person who'd lived and existed and died shook her in a way she couldn't explain.

He'd been hers, though, hers alone, and for that she was thankful. She just wished he didn't have to die. Tippy Trinkle probably knew this feeling better than anyone. After all, he was her brother. Who was Agatha to feel sad about 'losing' him again? Is this what growing up felt like? If so, she didn't like it.

She opened the drawer to her nightstand drawer and grabbed her jewelry box which housed rocks and shells and beads and no jewelry. It also housed the piece of paper from the Deer Island Ghost, and she knew this paper from Big would be two more lines of some sort of poem. She gently unrolled both pieces of paper until they lined up, four succinct little lines that, when complete someday, Agatha knew would be a clue of utmost importance:

I'm sometime where the old men chat
With big cigars and fancy hats
Where feet get warm and fingers tingle
Where good friends often meet and mingle

Agatha read the words aloud to herself several times. It was a place, for sure, but who knows what she would find there once she figured out where 'there' was. She rolled both pieces of paper back up and placed them back in the box, putting them away for now. She knew not to put too much thought into it as several more clues would be given to her with new assignments.

Agatha decided to text Tippy to check in.

You ok? Agatha shook her head at her wording. That's not really what she wanted to say. In fact, she had a lot more to say to Tippy Trinkle, but that would be for another time, if ever. The response came immediately.

Yes. I feel better. If that's how you put it? Better. Normal. Whatever. It's like everything is undone. Does that make sense?

Agatha didn't understand. *I guess. What do you mean by undone?*

I mean, like reversed. Anything Henry did is gone. Notes he left me and stuff. All gone. Weird. How did you do it? And....thank you.

Agatha quickly shut her phone, shame filling her entire being, hot and heavy and cumbersome. She hadn't done anything. Leopold had. But what?

Suddenly, she had an idea.

"Hello?" Aunt Letty said when she answered Agatha's phone call, breathless.

"Are you ok?"

"Yes, honey," her aunt paused to take a couple breaths. "Whew. I was trying to move that wardrobe, but I'm going to need you and Tobie to help me. It hardly budged."

Agatha didn't agree to it. She wanted to avoid touching the wardrobe. "Um, Aunt Letty, do you still have your little book? The J. Wiltz one, I mean."

"Of course."

"Can you check something in it for me?"

"Like?"

Agatha paused. "Um.... the epilogue."

"What? That's torn out."

"Can you see if it's.... STILL torn out?"

"Do you mean it might've magically reappeared?"

"Yes."

She heard Aunt Letty let out a little chuckle. "Hold on."

A few minutes passed while Agatha waited. *A little too long*, Agatha thought. She was about to hang up when her aunt came back to the phone.

"Agatha?" Her voice edged with bewilderment.

"Yes?" she shouted into the phone, too eagerly. "I'm sorry. I mean, yes?"

Aunt Letty cleared her throat. "It's...it's here."

CHAPTER 44
NERDS

Agatha's heart did a triple flip. "What does it say?" She gnawed at the inside of her cheek as Aunt Letty began to read.

"How is it here? Oh, nevermind," Aunt Letty changed her mind on her question. "Funny, the 'Notes on Deceivers,' or well, the epilogue, is only one page. Just a single paragraph."

"Just a paragraph?"

"Yes," Aunt Letty said. "Are you ready?"

"Mm-hmm," Agatha mumbled, her thumb now in her mouth.

Aunt Letty began to read.

"Only an Oracle, often referred to as a 'Light,' has the power to immediately destroy a Deceiver. He/She has this capability but with

one caveat: They do not have to. And Perceivers should beware. While they can assist and do good things, most Lights are natural tricksters and require persuasion in the form of payment for their services of destroying Deceivers. Forms of payment can be given only by Perceivers and are usually one of two things: an act of love or a sacrifice."

She heard her aunt close the book, but she said nothing. *A sacrifice.* Agatha felt sick. "Thank you, Auntie," she managed to say as she hung up, making no effort to correct herself by calling Aunt Letty 'Auntie.' Agatha touched her abdomen, its contents and juices lolling and rolling around the little pink sack that formed her stomach. She needed air.

Her bedroom window pried open with a small groan, and the evening air hit her face, nice and chilly and spotted with moisture. It was drizzling. She inhaled with her eyes closed, constantly seeing Leopold's face which she tried to shoo away amidst the tears. What had he done? Where was he? Was he coming back? He'd solved her problem for her, but she didn't want him to! She wanted Leopold, even if that meant having the Deceiver still here, still present, still causing problems. How could she figure anything else out on her own? She still had other assignments coming, she knew, and Leopold had always been a fixture in her adventures. Her friend, her confidante, her comfort. Agatha squeezed a few tears out of her eyes and rubbed them, staring at the headstones in the distance.

The breeze blew in her face again and her eyes came to rest on something caught in the window frame. There, wedged in the wood was a piece of paper folded like some sort of bird. She gasped and popped the screen off her window, crawling out until her socks hit the mushy ground outside. She snatched the piece of paper knowing full well who it was from. How long had it been there? The rain had moistened it, and she hoped Leopold had written in ink that wouldn't run if wet.

The corners of the folded paper easily unfurled to reveal the same paper with the dark crow in the corner as the one he'd left his mother. The rain hadn't erased his words, and Agatha stifled a cry as she saw Leopold's handwriting.

Dear Agatha,

Go to where we first met and I said the word 'diarrhea.'

PS. It's always been Lucius.

Agatha flew through her backyard, scaled the fence, and rushed to her uncle's grave in the rain, her socks clumpy with mud that squished between her toes. She stood before the Ainsworth mausoleum where just a few months prior, she and Leopold tried to guess how the child in the crypt had died. Agatha could hear Leopold in her brain. "Diarrhea," he'd said, before blushing bright pink.

Agatha circled the crypt until she came to the side, and just as she'd suspected, an envelope was impaled by one of the grave's pointed fence posts. It, too, was wet, but Agatha was gentle upon opening it, standing in the rain and darkness to read Leopold's words to her.

The first few papers were printouts of articles about Lucius Nikolai, the same ones she'd seen earlier on Tobie's laptop. Leopold had highlighted certain parts of the article, namely the word 'light,' which Agatha now understood. The name of Lucius Nikolai's former funeral home had also been highlighted, a nugget of importance Agatha had missed. "Eternal Light Funeral Home." She bit her lip.

Light.

The third piece of paper was a printout of a name search Leopold had done. Agatha shook her head in amazement.

"Lucius" name meaning: Lucius derives from the Latin word Lux, meaning "light."

The final piece of paper in the envelope was again the stationery with the crow, and Leopold had scrawled his final message for Agatha. He'd started with the Martin Luther King, Jr., quote:

"Darkness cannot drive out darkness; only light can do that. Hate cannot drive out hate; only love can do that."

Agatha,

THERE ARE TWO REALMS: The Living and the Dead.

I believe Aunt Hattie is trapped over there, and I'm going to find her.

Know this: Your aunt isn't lost, and neither am I.

(I'll probably come back as a cat like she did, but I hope it's something cooler.)

Watch for me!

Nerds always find the answers.
Leopold

Agatha fell to her knees in front of the Ainsworth crypt, Leopold's note held so tightly between her fingers she hoped it would become part of her. She squeezed her hands together and started to cry, the rain intermingling itself with her salty tears. She stayed that way until her dress was drenched and clung heavily to her body, making her small frame shiver in the night. She clutched the papers to her chest as she climbed to her feet, walking in a daze back to Azalea Drive, completely skipping her home and heading to the empty lot across from Leopold's house.

The sky was electric and the thunder rumbled as Agatha Anxious found herself standing in front of Leopold Panic's bedroom window. His mother's car was not in the carport, and Agatha suspected she'd found it too difficult to remain at home for the time being.

Agatha stared at his bedroom window for a long time, her heart hardening with the sort of anger that spurns focus, resolve, and determination. She glared at the darkened room beyond the windowpane, empty of the soul she called friend, and made a vow as she pressed her wet hand to his window. She whispered a few words into the night and then headed home to her own bedroom, climbing back through the window.

She tore off her wet dress, throwing it in a sloshy heap in the trash can by her desk. She grabbed the pair of jeans her mother had laid on her bed, neatly folded with the tags still on in case they didn't fit and needed to be returned, but Agatha decided they would work no matter what. She ripped off the tags as she slid her thin legs into the jeans and pulled them up where they fit nice and snug. She threw on a t-shirt that was too big and knotted it around her waist, her jaw still clenched from the last hour's events.

From her closet, she pulled down Aunt Hattie's golden box, gently lifting the lid and pulling out Blanche Caillavet's handheld cat mirror, its angry cat face scowling at her, daring her to add another piece of glass to it.

Agatha scowled back and obliged, placing the shard Big had given her into the broken frame where it was a perfect fit. Agatha wrapped the mirror in newspaper and placed it back into Aunt Hattie's box, shutting her closet door and this chapter of her Perceiver adventure. Was it an adventure anymore? This was no longer fun, Agatha thought. And it felt much more like a duty.

Three more to go.

She decided to sleep in her jeans. After all, they were surprisingly comfortable. She slid her hand in and out of the pockets several times. It was something she'd long wanted, pockets, but she didn't smile. Agatha looked up to find HattieCat watching her from the doorway, her long tail wrapped tightly around her body and laying over the tops of her paws. Their eyes met briefly in a mutual understanding of pain and torment.

Agatha Anxious knelt before the white cat with the black spiral on its chest and placed her hand in the fur of its back.

"I won't say her name, Auntie," Agatha said. She pressed her forehead to the cat's face and hissed her next words through gritted teeth. A venomous promise with all the makings of revenge.

"I am going to destroy her."

EPILOGUE

"Get up." Tobie nudged Agatha on Sunday morning. "We have to go to Mom's."

"Hmm?" Agatha said, her head under her pillow.

"She needs help moving some dumb dresser. And we have to get Macbeth remember? He's still over there."

"Mmm," Agatha groaned. The wardrobe.

"Are you wearing jeans?"

Agatha waved him away as she sat up, her hair frizzy from a tumultuous sleep. A melancholy misery returned to her heart, knowing the prior evening's events were real and not something she could chalk up to being a nightmare. Leopold's room was still empty. Aunt Hattie was still a cat. Agatha still had ghosts to help. That last part was ok. The other two were not.

She jumped out of bed and joined Tobie in the truck a few minutes later. He offered a breakfast bar. She shook her head.

"This won't take long," he said, as if that was the reason for Agatha's sadness.

"You ok?" he said finally, after fifteen minutes of silence.

She nodded, thinking for a few minutes. They were parking in Aunt Letty's yard when she decided to answer him. "I have a lot of stuff to tell you. Ghost stuff. And you're just going to have to get over that 'not believing' crap when I do."

Tobie's eyes widened, large chocolate circles and he blinked a few times exaggeratedly. A small chortle exited his lips. "And why is that?"

Agatha yanked the door open. "Because I need your help and you're all I've got."

Aunt Letty greeted them at the door along with Macbeth who seemed ready to go, with his heavy panting producing drool out of both sides of his mouth.

"You want anything to eat?" Aunt Letty said, pouring herself a cup of coffee.

"Nah," Tobie said. "Where are we putting the dresser?"

"You know, I think I'm going to get rid of it."

"Really?" Agatha piped in.

"Yeah. Should I not?"

"No, you definitely should," Agatha said. "I hate that thing."

Aunt Letty smirked, leading them to the back room. "Yeah, me too. It was your grandmother's and it's just creepy. I don't like creepy."

Agatha nodded. "Exactly." She'd had quite enough creepy lately and knew there was more to come. But if it meant the wardrobe was going away, Agatha was happy to help.

"Hang on, I left my coffee in the kitchen. Be right back." Aunt Letty headed back down the hallway calling for Macbeth.

Tobie and Agatha stood in silence in the room staring at the wardrobe. He opened one of its doors, revealing an empty space. Aunt Letty had removed all of Agatha's grandmother's clothes at least. Nothing to look at. Agatha placed her hands on one side of it just to force herself to touch it.

"Looks like somebody drew or colored in here," Tobie said, poking his hand inside the wardrobe.

"Colored?"

"Chalk or something. Look." He pointed to the back piece of wood where a lone white spiral was drawn and an arrow next to it, pointing down. "Doodles, I guess."

Agatha rolled her eyes at Tobie. "See, this is what I'm talking about. We need to get your third eye working."

"Huh?"

Agatha poked around the sides of the wardrobe and the bottom piece but found nothing. She reluctantly lay on her stomach and ran her fingers on the underside of it until her hands felt a knob. She pulled it and it shifted to the left. A small compartment revealed itself and inside, a book. Agatha sat up. Dried, pressed flowers adorned its cover with several spirals drawn around the flowers. In the bottom righthand corner of the cover was written "HMA," which Agatha immediately recognized as Aunt Hattie's initials.

She sat up, the book in her hands and looked up at Tobie, bewildered. His expression mirrored hers.

Dust blanketed the cover of the journal, and it creaked, begrudgingly, as she opened its pages to a random page of the book. Agatha's eyes started to water as she read the haunting message in the script of a fourteen-year-old Hattie Anxious:

October 9th

I am not sure I can help this ghost.

She is very angry, and I don't know why.

And I am afraid.

ACKNOWLEDGMENTS

Many thanks to my advance readers: Sarah Ainsworth, Mandy Hester-Sarrubbo, and Rachel Lovingood. Your laser focus helped transform this book into something richer than I imagined, and I am fiercely proud of it. Thank you for honing every whisper in the dark, every hush among the headstones, and every shadow lingering in the morgue.

For my publisher, Mark, and my cover designers, Diana and Patience--thank you for your guidance and creative expertise, and for your help ushering this book into the world, whether into the light of day...or perhaps the dark of night. We really did a thing.

I am endlessly grateful to young readers who love a good shiver, for their bravery of being spooked but turning the page anyway. And for the librarians, teachers, and booksellers who place these creepy stories into eager hands, I am eternally grateful.

Finally, for anyone who's ever felt a little bit different, insecure or anxious, this book is for you. But most of all, The Deadfellow Five series is 100% FOR THE NERDS. I'm one myself, and I love every last one of you. (If you don't understand, read the books!)

ABOUT THE AUTHOR

RJ MCDOWELL grew up in Biloxi, Mississippi, with a vivid imagination and an imaginary friend, both of which followed her into adulthood. She adores all things spooky and pens her creepy stories by candlelight. She lives in a house she calls McDowell Manor, where she eats black licorice and is still afraid of the closet monster. She hopes her readers like the dark as much as she does.

www.ingramcontent.com/pod-product-compliance
Lightning Source LLC
LaVergne TN
LVHW091130080826
845145LV00008B/2105
9781954798380